What

It must be something to do with the ~~~ if so, Sky should know about it. Not that he expected her to tell without some convincing. He could convince her, though, if he put his mind to it.

Curled on the couch, Pippa appeared so vulnerable. Maybe that's why he hesitated. His softer side wanted to sidle up next to her. To take her in his arms. To make her feel safe.

Trouble was, she wasn't safe from him.

Eventually, she would learn his identity and realize what he wanted of her. Then she would no doubt hate him.

Not that he should care.

He would never complete his mission if he let conflicting feelings get in the way. And then he would never know the truth. He needed to get close to Pippa McNabb, but if he started caring about her, it would only mean trouble—for both of them.

Dear Reader,

At the first nip of crisp fall air, I begin my countdown to Christmas. The high point is the annual Pinianski-Majeski Fete—Pinianski being me, Majeski my husband Edward—a tradition among our friends and relatives. I'm not certain whether they think it's great or whether they indulge me because they figure I'm a perennial child at heart.

Everyone knows kids like to be naughty, right? And how much naughtier can I get than to kill off Santa Claus…twice! If I didn't have such affection for all the trappings of the holiday, the dastardly deed wouldn't be such fun. I killed off my first Santa in *Crimson Holiday*, which you made one of the most popular Harlequin Intrigue books ever. And in *Crimson Nightmare*, I decided to "Return to the Scene of the Crime" as part of Harlequin Intrigue's Tenth Anniversary celebration.

I hope when you close the covers of Pippa's new story, with Sky Thornton, you'll have had a few laughs, a few tears and even more thrills!

Patricia

Patricia Rosemoor

Patricia Rosemoor

Crimson Nightmare

Harlequin Books

TORONTO • NEW YORK • LONDON
AMSTERDAM • PARIS • SYDNEY • HAMBURG
STOCKHOLM • ATHENS • TOKYO • MILAN
MADRID • WARSAW • BUDAPEST • AUCKLAND

To Linda Sweeney, for the eight tiny reindeer

And thanks to the Lincoln Park Zoo, for personalizing
Lapland's beast of burden for me

ISBN 0-373-22291-2

CRIMSON NIGHTMARE

Copyright © 1994 by Patricia Pinianski

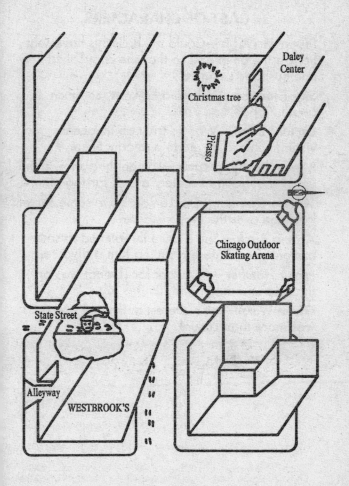

CAST OF CHARACTERS

Pippa McNabb—Could the holidays have sent her off the deep end so that she copycatted her late husband's murder?

Sky Thornton—Why did he know so much about Pippa?

Lamont Birch—Was he truly an innocent victim...or had he made a deadly enemy?

Mayor Darby Keegan—Lamont had shown him up as a buffoon at society events far too often.

Valerie Quinlan—Did Lamont have some secret leverage over the mayor's aide?

Acacia Birch—She'd once threatened to see Lamont dead before granting him a divorce.

Frank Hatcher—His work for Lamont was on the side and might cost him his job.

Gwen Walsh—Her interest in Lamont's records was more than casual.

Prologue

What was supposed to be a heartwarming holiday was turning into a crimson nightmare.

Peace on earth, goodwill to men?

Bah, humbug!

Christmas should be a time for loved ones to draw together not only in body but in spirit, as well. A time for children to anticipate Santa's bounty. A time for adults to forget their worries and concentrate on revitalized hopes for the coming new year.

It wasn't supposed to be like this.

Days filled with hate. Nights filled with fear. Being eaten away by thoughts of revenge.

Revenge.

Only if done superbly—without conscience—would it mean an end to the hate and the fear.

Looking around the crowded room filled with people of good cheer... listening to the music heralding Santa's arrival... the solution seemed almost obscene. But there was no other way. It had to be done.

One of the partygoers was about to receive an

early Christmas present—a crimson nightmare of his very own.

Then, for others, there would be real reason for a holiday celebration.

Chapter One

"Something's burning." Connie Ortega, catering manager, poked her head out of the commercial-size refrigerator to singsong the warning.

"Oh, no, my appetizers!" Heart thumping, nose quivering at the unpalatable smell, Pippa McNabb left the silver tray she was filling with fresh shrimp on toast triangles and ran for the oven. She whipped open the massive door and released a thick black fog into her face. "Yuk!" Coughing when she accidentally inhaled some smoke, she waved her arms and backed up. "They're ruined!"

Connie slammed the refrigerator door and gave her one of those soul-shrinking looks she was famous for. Considering Pippa had been working in the catering department for nearly three weeks now, she was getting used to Connie's disapproval. Oh, well. She'd never professed more than a passing acquaintance with kitchen appliances.

"Go ahead," Pippa told the catering manager, who had merely returned to the kitchen to take another full cart down to the party. The rest of the staff were still on the first floor, working the Christmas fund-raiser for the Coalition to Feed the Homeless, which would provide food for the entire holiday weekend. "I'll just get another batch of empanadas out of the refrigerator and into the oven and be down as soon as they're baked."

"You're the boss." Connie slipped something Pippa couldn't see onto her cart and made for the service elevator.

And Pippa pondered the irony of those words while trashing the blackened appetizers.

Indeed, she was the boss, by virtue of having inherited half of Westbrook's Department Store from her late husband, Dutch Vanleer, who'd traded pro football for merchandising three years before. Not that she was exactly competent to be in charge of anything. She'd married Dutch straight out of college, and he'd never allowed her to work while he was alive. That's why she'd left the running of the business to Dutch's and now *her* partner—her brother, Rand McNabb— while she tried to learn the store's inner workings, one department at a time, switching to a new venue on the first of every month. So far, she'd finished stints in lingerie, women's sportswear, shoes, small appliances, leather goods, china, men's accessories, toys, books and cosmetics.

None had proven to be a disaster until she'd switched to catering.

So what had she expected? Dutch had always disparaged her attempts at cooking and had insisted on frequenting restaurants and relying on hired cooks or catering services for dinner parties. Quickly placing the half circles of dough filled with turkey in mole sauce on clean baking trays, Pippa tried to push the mostly unpleasant memories of her late husband from her mind, but the attempt was futile.

The holidays were here again, after all, and the anniversary of Dutch's death was right around the corner. He'd been unofficially playing Santa, intending to somehow seduce Shelby Corbin—now Shelby Corbin McNabb, her brother's wife—into playing with him. Instead he'd been murdered, right here at Westbrook's.

A chill swept over Pippa, despite the heat of the oven, as she slid in the last of the canapes. She shook away the odd feeling and went back to filling the silver tray, which she then set on the cart she herself would take downstairs. No reason to worry. She'd already experienced one unforgettable crimson holiday.

Given that, things could only look up.

SKY THORNTON VAINLY looked for a woman with bright red hair amongst the holiday crowd. Standing out in the crisp snowy night, ignoring the soft snorts and restless clopping behind him, he continued to stare through one of Westbrook's State Street windows. Inside, Chicago's royalty was gathering to spread their largesse among the needy... as well as to be seen and photographed for the morning newspapers' society pages. No homeless among them spoiling the festivities, that was for damn sure.

He'd met a few of the partygoers since getting back in town. But most were strangers... only one of whom interested him. He'd seen *her* photograph enough times to recognize her.

So where was she?

His gaze traveled along a line of women in sequins and spangles, feathers and fur. Plenty of blondes and brunettes, but no redheads.

The costumed medieval carolers stationed on the corner behind him struck up a Christmas tune.

"Hark, the herald angels sing . . ."

Inside, the crowd blocking a rear elevator parted. Tuxes straightened and spangles rippled as people moved out of the way. Sky wryly told himself to be prepared to be impressed by whatever caused such a stir.

He damn well was awed.

The redhead he'd been looking for was pushing a catering cart toward a linen-covered table near the window. What was she doing working?

No glitz for her. Well, maybe a touch. A gold lamé, ribbon and bead-trimmed collar topped a full-sleeved winter white blouse and calf-length forest green skirt. And above the collar sat a mass of bright red curls. She'd attempted to hold them back from her face with a ribbon as green as her vivid eyes, but ringlets strayed beguilingly to rest against her milky complexion. One smooth cheek was marred by a dark streak—as if she'd swiped at it with a sooty hand. Her face was heart-shaped, her mouth bowed, her chin slightly dimpled.

He recognized her . . . and yet he didn't.

She was softer-looking than the photograph had indicated. Sweeter. Dare he say innocent? She could be a real Christmas angel. And he didn't like his instant and involuntary reaction to that thought.

He didn't want to like *her*—liking her would make his mission too tough.

"Hey, mister, you gonna give rides or what?"

Startled out of his private reverie, Sky turned to face a lanky street urchin in tattered clothing who glared at him in challenge. The youth's voice was barely in the process of changing, but he looked wizened, far older than his years. Poverty did that all too easily. Behind him, crossing kitty-corner from the outdoor ice-skating arena, were two younger kids—a boy and a girl, both too thin and both of whom appeared afraid to expect anything out of life other than another kick in the butt.

"Forget it!" the older one said when Sky didn't immediately answer. "He only gives rides to them that's got some mean green in their pockets."

Expression disgusted, the boy spun and quickly moved—until Sky's hand caught his upper arm, stopping him cold. "I don't like anyone putting words in my mouth."

"Yeah?" The young face turned, half hopeful, half suspicious. "You got better ones?"

Sky let go and indicated the waiting sleigh. "Get in. I don't have all night." The party guests who desired rides would be lining up for his services in a matter of minutes.

As the three youths screeched in glee and made a dash for the sleigh, Sky glanced over his shoulder and, for an instant, was caught despite himself.

She was there at the window, her eyes raised to the gently falling snow, a golden glow of candles and store lights behind her, haloing her copper hair and making her appear even more ethereal. Then her gaze lowered...to him. She blinked as if in surprise. Her mouth trembled into an unwary smile, and she lifted a hand in tentative greeting.

Sky's heart lurched before he cursed himself and turned away, blocking out his image of her and the sound of the heavenly chorus on the corner.

"Peace on earth, goodwill to men..."

He'd learned the hard way that people rarely had goodwill for one another unless it suited their purposes. He doubted Pippa McNabb would prove an exception.

PIPPA RELEASED THE BREATH she'd been holding when the driver jogged over to his sleigh. He moved like an athlete, as if running in the cold and snow was second nature to him. He seemed to be a powerful man, tall and broad shouldered beneath the brightly patterned wool jacket. The spill of hair from under his snow-dusted woodsman's hat was inky black. There'd been something electric in the way he'd looked at her, though his response hadn't exactly been positive.

He'd seemed...confused...almost as if he thought he should disapprove of her. Which, of course, was ridiculous since they were complete strangers. Watching the kids pile into the sleigh broadened her smile and made her think kindly of the man, anyway. He could just as easily have threatened to get a security guard as give the scruffy trio a ride. As the stranger slid into the driver's seat and gathered the reins, Pippa forced her attention back to the festivities inside.

A quartet started another cheerful Christmas melody. Standing nearby, Frank Hatcher, Westbrook's data processing manager, was checking his watch. A nervous little man, he always seemed to be concerned with the time.

"Ho! Ho! Ho! Mer-r-r-ry Christmas!" boomed a deep voice. Standing next to the giant Christmas tree that rose nearly six stories up the atrium, Santa Claus was handing out small tokens of the holiday—beautifully wrapped commemorative ornaments—to the benefit's attendees. Tall, stocky, silver-haired and in his mid-fifties, Lamont Birch made the perfect Santa. Westbrook's vice president of legal affairs also happened to be legal counsel for the Coalition to Feed the Homeless. Holding the fund-raiser in the prestigious department store had been Lamont's suggestion.

"Lamont, a word, please!" demanded his wife, Acacia. A stunning woman well past forty, she looked a decade younger despite the silver streak in her dark brown hair. Dressed in an elegant beaded red gown, she was supervising every detail as if the party were under *her* command, as if *she* rather than Gwen Walsh, the coalition's director, were official hostess.

And when, her expression grim, Acacia bent over to whisper something in her husband's ear, Pippa wondered what the problem might be. Above the fake white mustache and beard, Lamont's face darkened. Pippa drew closer but couldn't hear his muffled response.

Spine stiff, Acacia suddenly stalked off.

Before Pippa could decide whether or not to follow the woman and ask if there was anything she could do, Mayor Darby Keegan arrived with his entourage, including his blond, blue-eyed and very beautiful aide, Valerie Quinlan. Keegan was a celebrity spokesperson for the coalition. But, knowing the society lawyer and blue-collar mayor were sworn enemies—a matter of "have" versus "have-not" where class was concerned, according to Lamont—Pippa froze in her tracks. Surely the two men would make an effort to get along this one evening for propriety's sake.

But Mayor Keegan had been drinking. The glass in his hand was almost empty, and his bloated face was florid all the way up to his receding hairline. He looked revved up for a fight. "Hey, Santa, what ya got for me?" Keegan demanded. His manner was normally loud and officious, but tonight his words were slurred.

Heads were turning. Conversations were left hanging. Mouths were gaping. Pippa grimaced.

"Why do you need Santa Claus to give you anything, when you take whatever you want?" Lamont muttered under his breath. Aloud, he said, "A souvenir of the evening," and held one out.

Ignoring the offering, Keegan finished his drink. "Whose idea was it to make you Santa-for-a-day, anyhow, you shyster?"

Pippa tried to think of a way to cool this confrontation down, but Lamont quickly responded in kind. "Shyster? Me?" The lawyer laughed. "I'd be careful about slinging mud, if I were you, you money-hungry bureaucrat. One of these days your tactics will boomerang and you'll end up with mud in your face, as well you should."

Shock waves spread through the room. The two men were the focus of every eye and ear. Panicked that they might end up trading punches, Pippa acted on instinct. She grabbed a tray of appetizers and forced her way through the crowd toward the men.

"You got some problem with me, spit it out!" Mayor Keegan demanded.

"Mayor Keegan, please," Valerie Quinlan whispered from behind him.

"Oh, I shall," Lamont promised over her plea. "Though tonight's not the right time."

Lamont glanced beyond Mayor Keegan, his gaze stopping on the official's aide. Appearing horrified—by the proceedings or by Lamont's scrutiny?—the blonde took a step back right into the two aldermen behind her. The lawyer glared at his opponent.

"No, I want to savor the details a while longer, Keegan. Besides, we have more important affairs to attend to tonight. My accusations can wait until it's time to declare our candidacies for mayor—"

"Our? You think you got a shot goin' up against me?"

Pippa was now close enough to see the smirk curling Lamont Birch's lips when he countered with, "I think anyone with even a smattering of class would have a shot."

"Have an hors d'oeuvre!" Pippa commanded, and with an unusual display of authority for her, shoved the tray between the two men before they could get physical. "*Both* of you! They're small. Take *two*."

She glared from one to the other, silently demanding that they behave themselves. "Don't mind if I do." Mayor Keegan was known for being two-fisted whether he was running a campaign or eating, as his portly middle revealed. He proved it now, swaying as he scooped up a half-dozen delicacies in each hand. His famous "sincere" smile puffed out his full cheeks.

And the crowd released its collective breath. Party-goers turned away from the scene around the Christmas tree. Conversations gradually started up again. And Pippa heaved a sigh of relief.

Then she noticed Lamont was still glaring at the mayor. "Santa, try some of my appetizers." She leaned over and surreptitiously pushed the silver tray into his stomach padding until she was certain that she had his full attention. "Have one of each. I *insist*."

Grumbling under his breath, Lamont did as she commanded, snatching several appetizers without really paying attention to what he was doing. "Merry Christmas to all," he grumbled under his breath, "...and to all a good night. Except for *him*, of course."

But Mayor Keegan had already lumbered away and was lost in the swarm of people.

"Enjoy," Pippa said, moving on.

Her white face in contrast with her black hair and black velvet gown, her gray eyes as cold as slate, Gwen Walsh, director of the coalition, stood frozen nearby.

"Gwen, are you all right?" Pippa asked.

Gwen's odd expression indicated she hadn't realized she was the focus of anyone's attention. "I hope this ruckus won't affect contributions." She fussed with her French roll. "People are funny about needing to have faith in those who run organizations like the coalition."

While Pippa was distracted by a small group of people who wanted hors d'oeuvres, Gwen disappeared in the crowd. Pippa placed the empty silver server on a linen-covered counter.

"Spectacular save."

Hearing her oldest brother's voice behind her, she spun around as his wife added, "As good as any I've seen on a football field." Rand and Dutch had played for the Chicago Bears before retiring to buy Westbrook's.

"Where have you two been?" Pippa asked, glad for the company.

The soft look that passed between the two told her all she needed to know. Shelby's black hair was mussed, and there was a trace of her vivid red lipstick clinging to Rand's auburn mustache. No doubt they'd found some mistletoe. And who could blame them? They were still newlyweds, after all, having only been married for little more than six months.

"Never mind."

"We arrived in the midst of the fireworks," Rand admitted. "And couldn't get through the crowd. Sorry I was too far away to help."

"At least the situation was resolved," Shelby said, her hazel eyes bright. "I'm proud of you, Pippa. And, no matter what you say, I think you're ready to handle anything Westbrook's can dish out."

Heat rose along Pippa's neck. She admired Shelby greatly and equated that sort of compliment from her to getting a gold star. Too bad she didn't have the same confidence in herself that her sister-in-law did.

"Nothing surprises me where Darby Keegan is concerned," Rand was saying, "but this fund-raiser is Lamont's baby. What could he have been thinking of, baiting the mayor tonight?"

"I don't know, but something unusual is going on," Pippa told him. "It's like he was waiting for the mayor to show so he could sock it to him." The same chill that had swept through her in the catering kitchen returned.

"I'll see to it that nothing like that happens again," her brother promised.

"No more disappearing acts," Shelby added with a sigh.

"I'll make it up to you later, sweetheart."

"I'll see that you do." Shelby's lips bowed and her cheeks dimpled. "So let's mingle."

"See you later."

Pippa watched them take over the room. Both had a natural charisma that was hard to deny. Drawing in a deep breath, she tried to get her bearings, to figure out what to do next, now that she'd completed her catering duties. There would be cleanup later, of course. Meanwhile, she was starting to feel weird and not because of the argument. The Christmas music seemed louder, the smell of pine stronger, the tiny Italian lights strung throughout the spacious area brighter.

And the memories of a Christmas past began flooding through her.

Crimson memories. Of being informed that her husband was dead. Of weeping over Dutch's coffin, no matter how badly he'd disenchanted her those months before he'd died. Of being a suspect in his murder.

Murder and Christmas. The two didn't go together—or shouldn't, anyway.

Pippa scanned the room. Felt distanced from it. Felt chills shoot through her for a third time. She hoped she wasn't coming down with the flu. 'Twas the season.

Maybe she'd feel better if she retreated awhile. She could give herself a break. Just a few minutes off to herself wouldn't hurt anything, Pippa decided. She'd be back before anyone missed her. As she slipped through the crowd, images began to glaze over and sounds became muffled, giving the event a soothing unreality. The party was receding, the holiday becoming more removed. *Good.* Pippa convinced herself she was starting to feel better already. A walk in the alley by the loading dock would do wonders for her.

So when she passed a secluded recess of the room, where *Santa* stood arguing in a low voice—the recipient of his bad humor hidden by a support pillar—she turned her head away, determined not to interfere this time. Maybe he'd cornered the mayor. Or perhaps Acacia had cornered him—his wife hadn't been too happy with Lamont earlier. Whoever, Pippa didn't want to know. Didn't want to involve herself again.

So she sneaked away, out of sight, ignoring the scuffle and whatever hit the floor. Reminding herself that a few minutes alone couldn't possibly hurt anything.

LAMONT'S STOMACH HURT, but worse, he was having trouble breathing. Too much stress taking its toll on him, he reasoned. He was probably developing ulcers. And he really should have his blood pressure checked.

"Lamont, you're not looking so good," Rand commented, his amber gaze sharp.

"I'm not feeling too hot," Lamont admitted, turning bleary eyes toward the State Street exit. He didn't want to get in a discussion about what might be upsetting him. "Probably something I ate. Rich food doesn't always agree with me anymore. Not that I'm getting old."

"I can find you an antacid," Shelby offered.

"No. Thanks, but no. Getting some fresh air will do."

With that, Lamont lurched off, his gait unsteady as invisible hands began squeezing not only his windpipe, but his lungs, as well. He shoved at the revolving door and practically flew through it to the snow-covered sidewalk, where people were crowded in what seemed to be a line, despite the rapidly descending curtain of snow. He almost ran into one of them—a small man dressed like one of Santa's elves.

Who the hell was he? Lamont didn't remember anyone telling him to expect an assistant. He pulled his beard down, opened his mouth and gasped for air. His throat was closing rapidly. Suddenly panicked, realizing that he was in real trouble, he shoved through the crowd, trying to find a clear space where he could breathe properly.

"Pardon me, but the end of the line is that way," stated an elderly woman.

"Give Santa a break," her youthful companion suggested. "After all, that's *his* sleigh and team."

Though his vision was blurring, Lamont could see them coming through the thick veil of snow. He found himself poised directly on the curb. He was gasping now and waving his arms about to signal the driver. He had to get to a hospital and fast, and the animals looked like a racing team. But he didn't think the driver saw him. The team didn't slow.

Lamont put a hand to his throat and thought to yell with all his might when, suddenly, a solid blow behind his knee sent him crashing forward onto the icy street. People behind him screamed. A few plucked at his Santa suit to no avail. He felt the material rip.

And he heard the pounding of hooves.

Even as he turned toward the sound and tried to rise, he was kicked in the chest and fell onto his back. Pain struck him again and again—the moving, shifting weight knocking the last of the precious oxygen from his already abused lungs.

As the very life force drained out of him, Lamont couldn't help but recognize the irony of Santa Claus being run over by eight tiny reindeer.

In his head whirled the phrase: *Merry Christmas to all . . . and to all a good night!*

Chapter Two

"Whoa, Dasher, whoa, Dancer, Prancer and Vixen!" Sky Thornton yelled too late to prevent the impact. Still, he struggled to get the team under control as quickly as possible. "Whoa, Comet and Cupid and Donder and Blitzen!"

But the reindeer had momentum and couldn't avoid racing over the human who'd fallen directly into their path.

A roar of voices rose from the sidewalk. A piercing scream somewhere nearby made the hair on the back of his neck stand up. But by the time Sky had the animals in hand, the sleigh itself was perched atop the doomed man's chest—the vehicle holding not only his own weight, but that of Mayor Keegan, a member of the press and two aldermen. Half a ton had to be crushing the unfortunate victim.

"Get off now!" Sky yelled, firmly pushing the stunned-looking alderman sitting next to him in the other direction as he himself jumped to the ice-covered ground. He was already lifting the front of the sleigh even before the mayor, the reporter and the second alderman could scramble from the back seat. "Somebody help me!"

Several people responded, within seconds removing the sleigh from the man whose chest had to have been crushed by the weight—literally. Sky's assistant wrangler grabbed Dasher's bridle and led the team off to the side.

Santa remained absolutely still on the street. His eyes and mouth were fixed open in a blatant expression of horror. Blood bubbled out of his mouth and trickled into the white beard that had been pulled down crookedly to his chin, while a hoofprint stood out clearly in the middle of his forehead. More icy hoofprints added to the sleigh tracks that, literally, cut right through the Santa suit.

Horrified by the macabre sight, even knowing it was too late, Sky knelt on the frosty ground and tried to revive the man. Blood welled from Santa's chest through rents in the fuzzy red material of the costume. Though he got no response—not the slightest indication that Santa *could* be saved—Sky didn't give up trying until one of the guests identified himself as a doctor and took over.

Glad to give way, Sky nodded to his assistant and attempted to soothe the animals himself. Normally feisty in the wild, these reindeer had been hand raised and were semidomesticated. The small beasts were restless and quivering. Vixen made a mournful sound of distress, and Blitzen lashed out at the sleigh behind them. They were as unnerved as any of the humans present— just as he was, Sky thought.

The scene before him was unreal.

Sparkling, fluffy snow continued to dust the setting, giving Westbrook's that picture-perfect Christmas card look. But mere yards away lay a dead Santa. No doubt about it, he wouldn't be *ho-ho-ho*ing ever again. People dressed in finery, many without coats, multiplied along the sidewalk and began spilling onto the road, some speculating on what had happened, others complaining about their evening being ruined. Passersby were stopping to gape. A woman dropped her figure skates, and a man dressed as an elf rescued them. Photographers' bulbs were flashing and a roving video news unit, which had covered the fund-raiser for a local television station, was getting in position nearby.

"Stay back!" Mayor Keegan bellowed in his most officious manner the moment the video started rolling. "Keep the street clear."

His aide, Valerie Quinlan, had appeared out of nowhere, Sky noticed. One of those not wearing a coat, she was hugging herself and shaking as she watched the doctor's continued rescue effort.

"Mayor Keegan, can you tell us what happened?" asked the television reporter.

But Keegan's reply was cut off by the wailing of an ambulance arriving with a police escort. The cameraman turned away from the reporter to get a shot of the frantic activity as the paramedics came to the rescue, checking the victim for vital signs and consulting with the doctor who'd been working on him and who was now shaking his head sorrowfully. The older of the two uniformed cops approached him.

The younger cop looked around at the immediate crowd and flexed his authoritative muscles. "Someone wanna tell me what happened here?"

"Santa got run over by his reindeer!" a teenage boy said with a snicker.

His girlfriend punched him in the arm. "It isn't funny. They stomped him to death."

Having seemed unaware of the unique situation, the cop started and turned around. "All right, who's in charge of these savage animals?" he demanded officiously, tramping over to the sleigh and team.

Sky stepped forward. "I am. Name's Schuyler Thornton. And they're not savage."

"Then why did they *stomp* him?" the cop asked, indicating the covered body being lifted onto a stretcher, now the focus of the television and still cameras.

"Because he fell mere yards in front of the moving team and I couldn't stop them fast enough—"

"So you were driving the vehicle in question."

"That's right. I was giving the mayor and his entourage a ride—"

"I'm not involved in this!" Mayor Keegan blustered, obviously figuring he might somehow be blamed.

The cop narrowed his gaze on Sky, who was beginning to have an even worse feeling than being involved with a man's death had already given him. He glanced over at the paramedics, who were lifting their lifeless burden into the ambulance, and fought the uneasiness that twisted his gut.

"Cold night like this, a nip or two mighta seemed the thing to keep warm," the cop was saying. "Seems to me, a sobriety test is in order."

"You can give me any kind of test you want." Sky kept his voice even, though the implication that he had been irresponsible and, therefore, the cause of the bizarre accident made him furious. Bad enough that he blamed himself for not being able to anticipate the problem and not being able to stop his team in time. "I'm stone-cold sober."

"It was Santa who wasn't looking so good." A nearby stranger piped up in Sky's defense. "I think he was the one who'd had a few too many. Something was definitely wrong with him."

A woman volunteered, "He was kind of acting weird. Unsteady on his feet. But I'm not sure he was drunk. He seemed to be trying to get air or something."

Then the crowd parted and a tall, muscular man, whose dark reddish hair and mustache glinted under the streetlights, stepped through to the street. Sky immediately recognized the former player for the Chicago Bears.

"Lamont said he wasn't feeling well," Rand stated, backing up the witnesses. "That's why he came outside—for fresh air."

He glanced at Sky, but his expression didn't shift, didn't betray recognition. Not that Sky expected anyone present to know him.

"Poor man got more than he was expecting," the cop commented as the ambulance pulled away and his partner joined them. "And you are?"

"Randall McNabb, one of Westbrook's owners."

"So Santa was working for you?"

"Lamont Birch was, yes."

"I thought I'd seen it all," the older cop muttered. "What a way to die. Whose idea was it to bring wild animals onto the city streets in the first place?"

Those in the know looked toward Mayor Darby Keegan, who began sputtering, "An autopsy! I want an immediate autopsy. Something was wrong with Birch. Didn't you hear McNabb say so?" He turned to Valerie Quinlan, who looked nearly as frozen as an icicle. "See to it."

Sky figured the mayor wanted to make certain he was totally blameless and politically correct. The man that had been playing Santa hadn't been feeling well and, because of that, had fallen in front of the team—so his death was still an accident. What he couldn't figure out was why the mayor's aide seemed so totally out of it that it took a moment for his demand to register. Then she hugged herself even tighter and broke back through the crowd on the sidewalk, heading for the store, rushing as if she was trying to escape. . . .

By the time he turned his attention back to the cops questioning McNabb, two other women had joined the small knot of people on the street. Staring at the redhead who still looked every bit the part of a Christmas angel, albeit a very upset one, Sky reminded himself why he was there in the first place. If not for her, he would be far from this scene . . . and a man would still be alive.

In a roundabout way, Sky realized, unable to banish the dark thought, Pippa McNabb was every bit as responsible for Lamont Birch's death as he was.

ANOTHER CHRISTMAS PARTY, another dead Santa Claus.

Confused by the handsome sleigh driver's odd expression as he stared at her, horrified by the turn the evening had taken, Pippa felt like she was stuck in a bad dream.

A crimson nightmare.

She hadn't been able to believe her ears when, after taking that break to make herself feel better, she'd heard the dreadful news. In a tailspin, she'd run out of the store just as the ambulance drove off with Lamont's body.

"An autopsy does seem in order," the older policeman was telling the others.

"'Though, you ask me," added his partner, "the outcome's gonna be clear. No one coulda survived all that weight crushing down on him."

He glanced at the mayor, who began sputtering indignantly. And while the officers tried to calm Keegan down with assurances that he wasn't to blame in any case, Pippa found herself edging away from the hotbed of emotions.

"Dear Lord, I can't believe it's happening again," she murmured, glancing around to see the driver only a yard away, seemingly fixated on her.

She couldn't stop a flush from warming her cheeks. He appeared larger than life and even better-looking than she'd been able to tell from the store window. His eyes were pale, probably blue, and thickly lashed. His forehead was high, cheeks broad, jaw determined. There was something disturbing about him...vaguely familiar...especially about the full mouth that curled sardonically.

"Run into many dead Santas?" he asked.

Pippa started. So he'd heard her reference to Dutch's death. There was no way he could know about it, of course. Feeling as if her privacy had been invaded, anyway, she lifted her chin. "That's certainly a frivolous comment, considering a human being really did lose his life tonight." If she were a cruel person, she might add at *his* hands.

"I didn't mean to be disrespectful," the driver said, and only after a slight hesitation, added, "...to the dead man."

Pippa felt as if the stranger had slapped her. What reason would he have to be discourteous to her, though? Surely she was imagining that his hostility was personal. Perhaps he was equally unpleasant to everyone.

Or perhaps he was merely upset by what had happened.

She turned away from him, then felt his eyes burning into her back. Odd how he affected her, made her aware of his very presence even when she tried to put him out of her mind.

"Hey, you're shivering," Shelby said, moving closer and sliding an arm around Pippa's shoulders. "Let's go back into the store and warm up."

"Sure."

She'd be happy to escape the unfriendly sleigh driver, not to mention this numbing reminder of Christmas past...if only she could.

Just the year before, Dutch had been murdered while dressed in a Santa suit. Now Lamont. Of course, the lawyer hadn't been murdered, she reminded herself.

Shelby led her back through the crowd, saying, "I'll bet Mayor Keegan will curse the day he had the bright idea to use the sleigh ride as part of the fund-raiser."

Glancing back at the driver, whose broad back was to her while he tended his animals, Pippa asked, "Where did he find this guy and his reindeer, anyway?"

"I heard he was at Lincoln Park Zoo giving a special lecture and demonstration, which the mayor attended."

So, the stranger was more than a sleigh driver. Pippa was intrigued despite herself. A man hadn't gotten her attention so thoroughly since...well, since she'd first met Dutch.

She followed her sister-in-law through the revolving door back into Westbrook's and a disheartening scene. The area that had been a virtual sea of bodies a short time earlier was fast emptying. The coalition director, Gwen Walsh, was speaking to the musicians, who hurriedly began packing their instruments. The catering staff was already in the midst of clearing the counters that had been used to hold trays of food and drinks.

"Party's over," Pippa said despondently.

She spotted Acacia Birch, wrapped in her full-length fur coat and surrounded by friends, being led to a side door, undoubtedly to escape not only the crowd but the reporters. While holding herself stiffly, her expression properly sober, the new widow was not giving in to a display of histrionics.

"She's awfully calm for someone who just lost her husband," Shelby commented.

"People deal with grief in their own way." Though, when her own husband had been murdered, Pippa herself had been inconsolable for weeks, despite the fact that she'd been pursuing a divorce. "Maybe she's a private mourner."

"Maybe. Funny, she didn't even come out to the street to see for herself."

Pippa started. She hadn't realized. "Do you know something that I don't?"

"I'm merely being observant." But Shelby quickly changed the topic. "What a dismal result for a worthy cause."

"Hopefully, we made enough money on the tickets themselves to do some good," Pippa said, knowing the coalition director had been expecting some healthy donations, and equally certain that writing a fat check was the last thing on the mind of anyone still present.

Just then, Rand swept back into the store and put an arm around both women. "Time for the two of you to leave, wouldn't you say?"

"We can't go yet," Shelby protested. "How would it look if Westbrook's owners disappeared?"

"Besides," Pippa added without enthusiasm, "I have to help with the cleanup."

"I'm still in charge, right?" Rand asserted. "Then I say the two of you go home while I see to things around here. Pippa can stay at our place tonight," he said decisively, without asking whether or not she'd prefer company to being alone. "I'll call the limo while you two get your coats."

Once again her big brother was being overprotective, just as he'd been since they were kids—to which the scar decorating his cheek still attested. Sometimes the politics of their relationship annoyed Pippa, but not tonight.

"All right," she agreed, in truth happy that for one night she wouldn't have to face her huge, empty house alone.

As Vice President of Display and Communications, Shelby had an office right next to Pippa's, who used Dutch's old office between stints in the myriad departments. They headed for the elevators together.

"Don't be too long," Rand called after them.

"A few minutes," Pippa assured her brother.

But a couple of minutes stretched as long as her nerves when, after entering her office, she couldn't find her new green velvet cape. Upon her arrival earlier that evening, she'd come straight up here to secure her purse and to hang the garment in the closet. She swore she remembered doing so. Except for a change of clothing, the closet was empty. She looked around the office, just in case she'd dumped the garment on a chair or the leather sofa, but no hint of deep green velvet met her gaze.

"Hey, what's taking so long?" Shelby called from the reception area.

"No cape." Heels clicking on the parquet flooring drew closer. Pippa glanced at her sister-in-law, who stood in the doorway, coat draped over her arm. "It's gone."

"Are you certain you left it up here?"

"Positive."

"It couldn't have just disappeared. Your office was locked, right?"

Pippa's forehead wrinkled. "Oops. I was running late and didn't want to irritate Connie...." She could just about visualize a hanger in her hand but couldn't say the same about her keys. Crossing to her desk, she checked the drawer where she'd stashed her purse. It slid right open. "I guess I was in too much of a hurry." Thankfully, her purse was still there. Grabbing it, she slid the drawer closed.

"Still, even if you didn't lock the door," Shelby was saying, "would someone really have sneaked up here, taken your cape and left your purse?"

"Maybe the person wanted the cape for some reason."

Shelby swept her out of the office. "I think you're getting a little paranoid here. Where are your keys now?"

Pippa removed them from her pocket. Shelby pointed to the door and Pippa dutifully locked it.

"Now let's go find you something warm to wear home."

At least she had a department full of outerwear to pick from, Pippa thought, wishing that made her feel better. But something told her this wasn't the last she was going to hear about the missing cape.

"SOMEONE SPOTTED A WOMAN in an ankle-length hooded green velvet cape standing directly behind Lamont Birch when he keeled over into the street," Lieutenant Isaac Jackson told Pippa, Shelby and Rand first thing Monday morning.

In Rand's office, sitting directly across from one another on either side of the detective, Pippa and Shelby exchanged looks— Shelby's one of mild astonishment, Pippa's more of the I-told-you-so variety. Not that she didn't wish she could have been wrong.

"And the medical examiner found discoloration in back of the victim's knee," Jackson went on, "indicating someone probably kicked him there."

Pippa felt as if someone had kicked her. She already knew what to expect, even before Rand, ensconced behind his desk, asked, "So you think this woman in the green cape was responsible for Lamont's death?"

"Two and two usually add up to four." The homicide detective who'd handled the investigation of Dutch's death turned his liquid dark eyes on Pippa, who tried not to cringe. Friendly expression intact, he said, "I understand you own a hooded green velvet cape, Mrs. Vanleer. Can anyone verify your whereabouts at the time of Lamont Birch's death?"

"What?" Rand practically yelled.

"McNabb," Pippa corrected the detective, as invisible hands tightened around her lungs, making it difficult for her to breathe. "I went back to my own name after my husband's death. And, no, I don't have anyone to give me an alibi. I was alone."

"Alone where?"

"What is this, Jackson?" Rand demanded.

Pippa ignored her brother. "I took a short break is all. I wandered into the alley to get some fresh air and to think for a while. When I went back inside, Lamont had already had his . . . accident."

"Look, Lieutenant, so my sister has a green cape. Not exactly a unique item." Rand kept his tone reasonable. "As a matter of fact, Westbrook's is selling them this year."

Pippa suddenly realized she hadn't told him. "Mine was missing after the party, and I couldn't for the life of me figure out why someone would want to steal it. . . ."

Shelby backed her up. "I was there. It really was gone."

"Lost the cape," Jackson scrawled in his little notebook. "Convenient timing."

Pippa's mouth went dry. *Crimson memories.* It really was happening again. "You don't believe me?" The year before, Jackson hadn't believed she'd been innocent of her husband's murder, either.

"*Should* I believe you?" the detective asked.

"She has a witness," Shelby reminded him.

"To the fact the cape was gone, not what happened to it. If Miss McNabb was guilty, she would be smart to get rid of the evidence—give her *cape* an alibi, if not herself. And what about the victim's reason for going outside in the first place?"

"Lamont wasn't feeling well," Shelby stated, "as my husband told the investigating officers Saturday night. Maybe he was coming down with the flu."

Jackson shook his head. "More like something he ate."

"What? You think the food made him sick?" Rand frowned. "How could your medical examiner tell that?"

"Anaphylactic shock has some pretty obvious symptoms. He had a killer of an allergic reaction."

"You mean—" Pippa forced out the words "—something made by catering . . . killed him?"

Those dark eyes bore into her. "Something *you* insisted he eat. No one saw Birch touch any food all night except for the appetizers you forced on him after his argument with the mayor."

Pippa tried to stay calm even as she grew cold inside. "I didn't know Lamont had allergies."

"Furthermore, you stayed behind in the kitchen alone, giving you plenty of time to prepare a deadly canapé."

"I merely made more of some appetizers I burned!" Though she'd done nothing purposefully, Pippa felt oddly guilty. She gripped the arms of her chair. "Oh, no, maybe it *was* my fault."

"And maybe the reindeer and sleigh did him in, right, Lieutenant?" Rand urged, conjuring up an image of the driver for Pippa.

The way the stranger had looked at her . . . as if he'd thought her guilty of some crime . . . of Lamont's death? No, that was impossible. Something else had been eating at the man. And his reaction to her had been eating at Pippa since. She hadn't been able to get him out of her mind for long. According to the news media, his name was Schuyler Thornton, a naturalist who'd breezed into town with his reindeer only a few weeks before to start on some kind of lecture circuit based on his experiences in the wild.

"The medical examiner could not determine which circumstance was the actual cause of death," Jackson was saying, for the first time appearing discomfited. "Either way, he would have died, and intent—"

"But Pippa didn't know Lamont had allergies," Shelby told him.

"She could be lying."

"My sister doesn't lie," Rand insisted. "And Lamont should have been more vigilant about what he put in his mouth. Maybe he was more upset than anyone realized over his go around with the mayor. Maybe he got sloppy."

"And maybe someone had reason to want him dead." Those dark eyes were on her again. "Did you?"

Pippa started. "No! I hardly knew the man!"

"He worked for your company since last February."

"Lamont did legal work for some Bears players a few years back. I trusted Rand's judgment. Our relationship was strictly professional. I never got to know him well enough to dislike him...or to know anything about what he might be allergic to." Dreading the answer, she asked, "So are you going to arrest me?"

Jackson looked at her long and hard, his very silence pebbling the flesh up her spine.

"Not at this time," he finally said. "But you're not off the hook yet, Miss McNabb. Not by a long shot. I hope you weren't planning to get out of the city for the holidays."

Pippa would have dearly loved to get out of the city for some indeterminate length of time—like forever. But that would be the coward's way out. She might be foolish, gullible even, but she was no coward.

"My plans are to be with my family right here in Chicago."

"Good. See they don't change."

"What about Thornton?" Rand demanded. "What does anyone know about this guy, anyway? What if he was hired to be part of some elaborate scheme—"

Jackson interrupted. "He won't be leaving town any time soon, either."

With that, he terminated the meeting.

Her brother's insinuation stayed with Pippa. What if the sleigh driver had purposely run down Lamont? Her mind was whirling, and so when she took the elevator down, she missed the catering floor and went all the way to the first floor. Rather than riding back up, she wandered out, feeling shell-shocked, and was subsequently bumped by a dozen harried customers all trying to push their way in at once. The store had gone back to normal after the catered event. The entire floor was packed with holiday shoppers attacking accessory, jewelry and cosmetic counters with determination.

But holiday sales were the last thing on Pippa's mind.

Which had killed Lamont—an allergic reaction or being stomped by eight tiny reindeer? She must have given him the food that made him sick, the reason he'd gone outside in the first place. If he hadn't been outside...

Heavyhearted that she inadvertently might have been the cause of another person's death, Pippa found herself wandering toward the little-traveled area near the loading dock that split the first floor of the store in two. It took her a minute to realize why she'd come here. This was the last place she'd seen Lamont alive—in the dead-end recess near the pillar, where he'd been arguing with some person she hadn't been able to identify.

Someone who'd wanted him dead? Schuyler Thornton? Or someone who'd enlisted the stranger's aid to cover up the true cause of death? Had Lamont's death been the worst of all practical jokes or had he been murdered?

Until this moment, she hadn't remembered the argument. Not that remembering would have done any good, since she hadn't seen the second party. Lieutenant Jackson would have given her one of those looks of his that made her skin crawl. Standing there, staring at the vacant area as if it could provide some answers, Pippa felt the hair rise on the back of her neck.

Expecting to see the detective himself, she whipped around, but if anyone were watching her, she didn't catch him at it. The closest people to her were a runaway child and a mother loaded down with packages who came screeching after him. No sooner had the distraught woman jerked the toddler to a halt and headed him in the opposite direction than Pippa went back to her examination of the area—a curved wall and the back of a display case.

Her brow furrowed as she remembered something else about the incident the other night. A sound separate from Lamont's argumentative tone. Something dropping to the floor. Though she didn't expect to find whatever it was, since the fund-raiser area had been cleaned and put to rights the morning before, she took a careful gander. And though she didn't see anything right off, something made her look more closely.

Hunkering down, she inspected the baseboard along the curved wall. Nothing. Disappointed, she turned to the back of the display case and the open space beneath it. She reached in and felt around. Something skittered away from her fingers.

Without giving thought to the new suit she was wearing, she got down on her knees and reached under the display case, for a few moments playing tag with the article that had rolled underneath. She reached farther and felt the material of her sleeve snag. Finally, she was able to wrap her fingers around what felt like a rounded metallic object.

Sitting back on her heels, she stared down at the roll of film in her hand. Film? How peculiar.

She rose to her feet and dusted herself off, making a mental note to speak with the manager of custodial services.

Then she turned around, only to come face-to-face with the mysterious man who had been crowding her mind for the past thirty-six hours. The man who was as suspect as she. He looked tough—capable of anything. Murder, even? Against all reason, her pulse picked up and her breath became short... and Pippa recognized her reaction as fear mingled with something equally dangerous.

Soft jeans hugged the man's trim hips and muscled thighs and were tucked into waterproof mountain boots. His down vest was open, exposing the breadth of his chest covered by a pile turtlenecked pullover in a brilliant print of red, gold and blue. As she'd guessed, his eyes were blue, too. Deeply penetrating. And they were fixed on her as unnervingly as they had been the other night.

His full mouth curled into a mock smile. "Sky Thornton."

"Yes, I know," Pippa said, her own lips stiff. "You could have made yourself known earlier, rather than spying on me."

"I just got here this moment."

Having assumed his were the prying eyes that had made her hair rise a while ago, Pippa was taken aback. "Well, if you're looking for Lieutenant Jackson—"

"Not Jackson," he returned, the low timbre of his voice thrilling her against her will. "You."

Chapter Three

He had been looking for her—that was the truth. What he didn't admit was that he was ticked off because he'd been looking forward to finding her.

Her gaze was wary but steady. "What is it you want with me, Mr. Thornton?"

What didn't he want? Again her face was smudged, and he had to stop himself from reaching out to wipe it. Shrugging off his response to her as a result of involuntary abstinence—romance was hard to come by in the Alaskan wilderness, where he'd spent the past couple of years—Sky merely said, "To talk."

"About?"

"Funny, but I didn't get the idea you were dense."

Her gaze narrowed and her green eyes flashed contempt. "I certainly got the idea that you were rude, and you haven't disappointed me. Now, if you'll excuse me..."

She tried moving by him, but he shot out a hand and stopped her cold. "Not so fast."

"Let go of me before I scream."

She wrenched her arm, which he refused to free. She was captive and he was hardly making an effort. Sky tried not to let the fact bother him. "Do you really want to generate more bad publicity for your store?'' he asked. ''I don't think so.''

He could practically see the wheels turning in her head. Lamont Birch's bizarre death had been all over the papers both Sunday and this morning. And every local news show was following the story closely, due, no doubt, to the mayor's interest in clearing his name.

''My store?'' she asked, her expression questioning.

''You *are* Pippa McNabb, co-owner of Westbrook's along with your older brother Randall, right?''

Now she was looking at him with downright suspicion. ''What else do you know about me?''

''That you love football . . . and quarterbacks.''

Sky couldn't help himself. So it was a low blow. He was only a tad sorry that he'd made her lithe body and soft features stiffen. If she was the game player he'd been led to expect, he needed to stay one step ahead of her, to keep her off center. As horrible as the tragedy had been, Lamont Birch's death was going to help him do that at least.

''That's all in the past and has nothing to do with you,'' she said more calmly than he might have expected. ''*I* have nothing to do with you.''

But he could tell she wanted to. She was annoyed with herself for it, but she was interested. Good. That fit right in with his plans.

''Actually, you do,'' he said. ''Why don't we talk about it over a cup of coffee?''

He felt some of the tension drain out of the arm he was still holding. She nodded. ''All right. Downstairs.''

As they left the recess and rejoined the throng of people crowding the floor, he noticed her checking out a roll of film in her hand. What had that been doing on the floor? he wondered. When she realized he saw, she shoved it into her jacket pocket and speeded up toward the down escalator.

The sublevel floor was nothing like the old bargain basements that used to rest below the old department stores when he was a kid. Although low ceilinged, the area was bright and had been extensively and expensively redesigned, one department attractively giving way to the next. They passed books and small appliances. But upon approaching electronics, Sky once more put a hand out to stop Pippa when a bigger-than-life Mayor Darby Keegan stepped onto the screens of the myriad televisions on display.

Sky said, "Hang on. Let's see what His Honor, the Mayor, has to say to the news media."

Pippa didn't object.

"... true that the cause of death is not clear?" a reporter was asking.

Keegan's pale skin suffused with color all the way into his receding hairline. "Lamont Birch had a killer of an allergic reaction to something he ate at the fund-raiser. The medical examiner says it's doubtful he would have survived even if someone had gotten him to a hospital."

"But he might have survived if he hadn't been trampled?" an off-camera voice asked.

Sky shifted uneasily and glanced at Pippa, whose entire attention was centered on the mayor's response.

"Mighta, yeah. Not likely."

"But we'll never know that for certain," the reporter doggedly continued. "On the other hand, there was no way he could have survived being crushed by—"

"I tell you one thing for certain!" Interrupting the reporter, the mayor was practically shouting. "The police are gonna get to the bottom of this death. If there was foul play involved, the murderer is gonna pay. I won't rest until the person responsible for killing Lamont Birch is brought to justice!"

The news program cut back to the studio and Sky turned to go. Pippa stood there looking as stunned as if someone had smacked her, the smudge stark against a face as white as freshly fallen snow. Sky couldn't help himself. He had to fix it, after all. He gently cupped her cheek and rubbed at the smear with his thumb. Her skin was soft and smooth and inviting, making him yearn to explore more of her.

When she still stood there, frozen like a Popsicle, he asked, "Are you all right?"

Suddenly coming to life, she snapped away from his touch, and took a big breath...and a step back. "Sure. I'm fine." She didn't look fine. Hot spots of color flamed her cheeks. "Just fine," she muttered.

With that, she spun on her heel and made for the café, Sky following close behind, telling himself he couldn't soften toward her now. Reminded of his purpose, he waited until they'd ordered their gourmet coffees—hers flavored with hazelnut, his merely strong enough to grow more hair on his chest—before launching his attack.

"So Lieutenant Jackson got to you."

She started. "You seem to be awfully interested in my business."

"About that velvet cape of yours...does the green match your eyes?"

Those emerald pools opened so wide that Sky felt as if he could lose himself in them. He clenched his jaw and tried to control the male response that kept threatening to weaken his hand in this cat-and-mouse game.

"*You're* the one who told the police that someone in a green cape was behind Lamont when he fell?"

He shook his head. "I heard a witness from the crowd telling the officers about it the other night."

"So how did you know I owned a cape? How do you even know who I am?"

Unwilling to give her the edge with any part of the truth that wasn't necessary to divulge, Sky hedged. "Jackson interrogated me first thing this morning. He's not letting me off the hook until he has some concrete answers."

And Sky didn't like that one bit. Being held accountable for an accident was one thing, but being involved in a murder investigation . . . this was certainly a complication he hadn't counted on.

"Considering someone may have used me to take a man's life," he continued, "I'm interested enough to dig."

"Used you?" she echoed. "You mean me?"

"Did you?"

"No! I had no *reason* to kill Lamont Birch . . . even if I was responsible."

Now it was Sky's turn to be startled. "You're saying you *are* responsible for his landing in front of my sleigh?"

She stared down at her hands that she'd clenched into fists on the table. "I guess you don't know as much as you think."

"So enlighten me."

The waitress brought their coffee. Without adding anything to the strong brew he'd ordered, Sky took a big slug, enjoying the hearty taste that was so much more satisfying than the watered-down stuff he made in the wilderness.

"You know that killer of an allergic reaction the mayor was spouting off about?"

"Right, the anaphylactic shock."

"I'm the one who forced appetizers on Lamont and the mayor when they were going for each other's throat." Now she was gripping her mug so hard that her knuckles had gone white. "So in that respect, I was responsible for the allergic reaction . . . and ultimately for Lamont's death, since he went outside to get air because he was feeling so bad."

He hadn't heard this part of the story. Somehow her identity had been kept from the news media—the privilege of being co-owner of Westbrook's, a Chicago tradition? Sky wasn't certain how to take the information.

Could Pippa McNabb be even more devious than he'd been led to believe? Could she be a murderess?

Then she lifted her face to his. She looked guileless and far younger than twenty-nine, which he knew her to be. Staring into quickly reddening eyes swimming with unshed tears, Sky clenched his jaw against what could be an act. But his gut told him this wasn't playtime, that she was truly upset. That she felt as guilty as he did.

Maybe it was the lingering guilt that made him a bit cruel. "So what was it Lamont was allergic to?" he asked, his voice deceptively calm.

"How would I know?"

Sky merely arched his brows and took another slug of coffee. And watched her change from wounded to furious.

"What is the point of this conversation?" she demanded. "You trying to get the goods on me so you can exonerate yourself? Well, forget it! How do I know you didn't purposely run your reindeer and sleigh over Lamont?'' She sipped at her coffee as if that would calm her.

"I couldn't have known he would even be there." Sky hated sounding defensive. "Besides, *I* didn't even know who he was."

"A man in a fuzzy red suit would really be difficult to identify, right?" Her sarcasm was rife. "Did someone pay you to be on the lookout for him, and—"

"I never purposely hurt anyone or anything in my life. I'm a naturalist, not a hired thug!"

"And what does your insinuation make me out to be?"

Sky studied her for a moment then switched to a different tactic. "Look, I think we got onto the wrong footing with each other." If he made her too angry, she wouldn't give him the time of day. Then where would he be? "We're both on edge, both feeling a little guilty for something that wasn't our fault," he said reasonably. "I understand how upset you must be, since I'm under suspicion and I know *I'm* innocent."

Pippa distrusted this sudden change of attitude. Sky Thornton wanted something from her. But what? A confession? Nothing else made sense.

Staring at him harder, she tried to ignore the thrill that shot through her as their gazes connected and meshed, putting a lie to her easy conclusion. They were attracted to each other—angry, but attracted. That complicated things.

Then again, what if this was simply some weird come-on? The possibility made her uncomfortable. *He* made her uncomfortable. When he chose to, Sky Thornton could seem so . . . threatening. Even now, he leaned forward, elbows on the table, invading her space.

How had he learned about the cape? And about her love of football and quarterbacks? Since he supposedly had recently arrived in the area, how had he known about Dutch? She wondered if he'd had a single source for his information, or if he'd gone a lot of trouble to find out. Although he'd put on a pretty convincing act, she didn't believe he'd dug into her past to protect his own back.

Forewarned, forearmed. Perhaps she'd better find out what she could about him. "So where are you from, anyway?"

His surprise at her change in topic was obvious—as was his relief. For the moment, losing that tension that told her he was on the alert, he even slumped back in his chair.

"I'm not really from anywhere since I don't stay in any place too long," Sky told her. "I spent the past couple of years in Alaska and a few years before that in northern Minnesota."

"And before that?"

"The Upper Peninsula. Michigan."

He had the rugged looks that went with a rugged life. And yet, she sensed that that wasn't the life he'd been born to. "No roots anywhere?"

"I kind of lost touch with them years ago."

The fleeting emotion that he quickly hid told Pippa she'd struck a nerve. The question had definitely bothered him. Being part of a big Irish family herself, she couldn't imagine going through life alone. She and her parents and four older brothers and their wives and kids were all close-knit.

The words were out before she could stop herself. "How sad for you."

His jaw tightened and so did his tone. "Depends on how you look at it. Simply studying the behavior of wild animals from a distance can be more rewarding than trying to carry on sane relationships with people."

Pippa wondered if he'd been born cynical or if someone in particular had turned him that way. She figured probing deeper would put him off, and she wasn't through trying to get the skinny on him yet.

"So, who do you work for?" she asked, thinking of his reindeer. "The government? Or a university?"

"Myself."

She couldn't hide her surprise. "A naturalist who works for himself?"

"I've had a few articles published in nature magazines and educational journals over the years."

"Still, that can't be much of a living." Maybe he was independently wealthy.

"I live modestly," he said. "And being paid to take tourists out into the wild supports my habit."

Startled, she asked, "Someone who studies animals takes out hunting parties?"

Anger flashed across his features, and he slid forward, balancing both elbows on the table. "I don't kill animals, either," he growled. "I take people camping and hiking and canoeing. I teach them survival skills they couldn't learn in any city."

Pippa's pulse sang crazily. He looked as tough as any predator, and she had the sudden impulse to run from him as far and as fast as she could. A great believer in trusting her instincts, she forced her eyes to her watch. "Look what time it is. I have to get back to work."

"You're the boss. You can do what you want."

"Right. I want to set a good example."

Even so, it took Pippa a moment to stand, and then she had to contend with the slight wobble of her knees. Despite Sky's confusing attitude toward her, alternating between hostility and solicitude, she was fascinated—like a doe caught by a pair of bright headlights.

Or a reindeer.

"I thought you were in a hurry." Undoubtedly sensing her reason for hesitation, Sky seemed amused.

"I am." Awkwardly, she sidled away from the table. "It's been . . . interesting."

"It isn't over."

"Pardon?" Her heart gave an unwelcome thump . . .

"The investigation."

. . . and settled back down.

"Oh, right." She'd almost forgotten why he'd supposedly cornered her in the first place. "Hopefully, the authorities will decide it was all a horrible accident." Though that didn't seem likely. Lamont's eating something he was allergic to and being run over by a team of reindeer, both within the same hour . . . well, she wasn't that great a believer in coincidence. "There's really nothing we can do but sit tight and wait."

"That's a matter of opinion." At her questioning glance, he added, "We'll talk more later. I have some ideas on how we can speed things along. Don't worry, I'll find you."

She was certain he would. No doubt one of those survival skills of his was tracking.

Forcing herself to stare straight ahead as she moved toward the elevators, she cut through the growing crowd in the food court. Though she'd checked her watch only a few minutes before, the time hadn't registered. It did now. Noon. Lunch. She'd missed an entire morning in the catering department. No doubt when she did show, Connie would give her one of those looks of disapproval that made her cringe inside....

As Sky had so pointedly stated, Pippa reminded herself, she was the boss. And as such, she decided to return to her office to check things out before going on to catering. She gave in to the temptation to check Sky out one last time before the elevator doors closed, but he had already disappeared. Pippa fought down disappointment.

The executive level was unusually quiet. Everyone, it seemed, had opted to take lunch at the same time. Even the receptionist, Bridget, had stepped away from her desk for the moment.

When the silence was broken by the sound of a heavy drawer closing within one of the outer offices, Pippa figured Bridget was merely retrieving some work. About to continue on to her own office and check for messages, she hesitated when she realized the receptionist was in Lamont's office. Curiosity made her investigate... and surprise made her stop cold in the doorway.

The person rummaging through Lamont's things wasn't female. Though his narrow back was to her, she recognized Frank Hatcher immediately. The data processing manager was so intent on what he was doing that he didn't sense her presence.

"Oh, Ms. McNabb," came a familiar voice from the reception area. "Is there something I can get you?"

Pippa glanced back to see Bridget coming from the direction of the ladies' room and heading for her station. "No, nothing, thank you."

The receptionist slid behind her desk just as the telephone rang, and Pippa returned her attention to

Hatcher, who was facing her now, expression wary, back rigid, files clutched awkwardly in both hands.

"Good afternoon, Ms. McNabb." He forced the words through stiff lips.

"Are you going to tell me what you're doing in here?"

A flush crept up from his collar all the way to his thinning light brown hair. "Retrieving some data reports that I generated last week. Mr. Birch asked to get a gander at the material before I could finalize it."

Pippa wondered if she was imagining belligerence in his tone. "I see."

"I was supposed to come get them Friday, but I was too busy." He glanced at his watch and, clucking to himself, made a move to leave.

Instinct kept Pippa in the doorway a few seconds longer than necessary—long enough to block his speedy exit and get a clear view of the file folders. Then she stepped back and let the little man pass. Nerves atwitter, he practically flew by her in his rush to get away.

Getaway.

The thought echoed through Pippa's mind as she proceeded to her own office. Had Frank Hatcher been acting even more nervously than usual, or had she been imagining it? Her brief examination of the materials he'd retrieved hadn't shown her anything unusual. She'd recognized a few names—employees, some kind of personnel records.

Which she forgot all about the moment she entered her office and noted the morning newspaper, the front page of which boasted a photo of an angry Mayor Darby Keegan. She sat and scanned the article, which reiterated the politician's posturing to the television reporters. By the time she was done, she was cold inside. True, she might have inadvertently been responsible for

Lamont's death, but she didn't deserve to be jailed for what had been an accident. She didn't even know which canapé had done the deadly deed. A closer look at the article couldn't tell her, either. No mention was made of the ingredient that had done Lamont in.

Pippa didn't hesitate. Knowing how she could find out, she picked up the phone and called her father's precinct. He answered himself.

"Pop, it's Pippa."

"Hiya, sweetheart, howya holding up?"

The day before, her entire family had rallied around her, trying to mollycoddle her against bad memories of the previous holiday season. It had been one of those uncomfortable times when she'd both appreciated her loved ones and wished for a little distance.

"I'm fine. A little worried, though..."

By the time she finished telling him about Lieutenant Jackson's visit, her father was fit to be tied. His muttered curses shocked Pippa. She'd never heard her father swear before.

"You're under suspicion for murder *again!*" he raved. "What in blue blazes is wrong with that idiot Jackson? I'll have his badge—"

"Pop, take it easy."

"What easy? I been a cop for nearly forty years. I raised my kids to be law-abiding citizens! After the Dutch thing... Jackson should know better by now."

For some reason, Pippa found herself defending the man. "He's only doing his job. And speaking of jobs, maybe you could use a little of your influence to get me some information."

She shifted in her seat; something hard poked her in the hip, making her wince.

"You name it, sweetheart."

Reaching into her jacket pocket, she pulled out the roll of film she'd found earlier . . . and then had forgotten.

"Pippa?"

"Oh, sorry, Pop. Can you get me a copy of the autopsy report?"

Considering Jackson hadn't mentioned anything about the contents of Lamont Birch's stomach, she was certain he wasn't going to share the information unless forced. Thankfully, her father quickly agreed, and Pippa concluded the conversation by giving him her love and sending the same to her mother.

For a moment, she stared at the metal canister, wondering what the odds might be that a murderer had dropped it. Reaching for the telephone to call Lieutenant Jackson, she stopped herself. He thought she was guilty and would rather point a finger than share information, so why should she be so anxious to share this with him? He would probably pooh-pooh the idea of the film being possible evidence and ignore her, anyway.

On the other hand, she could have the film developed herself right after work and see what tales it might tell.

That decided, Pippa threw the roll to the back of her top desk drawer and was careful to lock up when she left. No sense taking any more chances.

Heading for catering, she thought about Sky Thornton's indicating they could speed the investigation along themselves. The question was, did she trust him enough to share what she'd found?

PIPPA MCNABB HAD FOUND the roll of film!

"Need some help, honey?" a brash young saleswoman asked.

Valerie Quinlan blinked and stepped back from the eye shadow display. "Oh, no thanks. Just looking."

Valerie had been wandering through the department aimlessly—trying to figure out what to do—ever since she'd spotted the roll of film in Pippa's hand when she'd left with the sleigh driver.

"Yeah, you and everybody else," the petite brunette mumbled half under her breath. Rolling her eyes, the saleswoman quickly moved toward another customer checking out blushes.

And Valerie was left to her racing thoughts.

What did Pippa McNabb plan on doing with the damn film and who else knew about it? If the mayor got wind of its very existence, the game would be up. And hadn't she tried to prevent that the only way she knew how? Not that anyone could necessarily figure things out, even if the film was developed. A picture might be worth a thousand words, but only if you knew the significance of what you were looking at. And surely that was impossible, right?

But was that a chance worth taking? Some people liked to dig and dig and would never stop until they had the truth.

Look what had happened to Lamont.

The truth could kill Pippa McNabb, as well.

Chapter Four

"Didn't think you were going to make an appearance today, after all," Connie Ortega commented as Pippa finally arrived in the catering department. The manager had wedged a hip on the desk in the hallway outside the kitchen. She was checking over some paperwork.

For once, Pippa didn't let Connie's typical nervy remark get to her. "I'd say a man's death takes precedence over my learning the business." She had to start standing up for herself or she would never be an effective store executive, no matter how many departments she tried to master.

To Pippa's surprise, Connie sobered and set down her clipboard. "I should have figured that's what was holding you up. So what's the scoop?"

While they didn't stop what they were doing, several other catering workers in the kitchen rubbernecked in their direction. No doubt speculation about the lawyer's death was running rampant throughout Westbrook's.

"Something we made in this kitchen didn't agree with Lamont," Pippa informed them all.

"What?"

Now every eye in the room was on her, and Pippa had to reiterate her earlier conversation with Jackson ... leaving out his insinuations of her own involvement. That information would become rumor soon enough. Even with half the story, the staff became suitably stirred up, and Connie had to redirect them off the subject and back to work.

Removing her suit jacket, Pippa hung it on a peg opposite the doors that led into the main store, then wrapped a full apron around herself. "What can I do?" she asked, thinking Connie looked kind of strange, as if she wasn't feeling well.

"I need you to check on some inventory for a political PR luncheon day after tomorrow. I just found out about it a few minutes ago." She took a deep breath. "Your brother said Mayor Keegan decided he needed some good press after what happened the other night. Why he would want us to cater it, though—considering what you told us—is rather odd."

Pippa also thought the decision was pretty strange. "Maybe he had the idea before he got the results from the medical examiner's office."

"Most likely. Even though we'll most likely have a cancellation, we'd better be prepared." The manager picked up the clipboard and handed it to Pippa. "I've marked the products I'm not certain we have enough of."

"I'll take care of it right away."

Connie scrabbled around the top of the paper-strewn desk as if searching for something. "I have a final meeting with the head of women's wear about a high tea for some new designers' representatives she's made deals with for the coming year, but I won't be long."

Muttering something unintelligible under her breath, Connie finally grasped a pad of lined paper that had been in plain sight all along and quickly exited into the store. Pippa figured the other woman was worried because her department had been implicated in Lamont's death, so she didn't dwell on the manager's unusual behavior.

She set off down the long hallway, trying to ignore the enticing smells of Christmas cookies and cakes wafting from the kitchen—her only lunch had been that coffee she'd shared with Sky—giving the list in her hand a quick once-over. The dozen or so ingredients in question were marked clearly with red checks. Shouldn't take more than a few minutes.

The storeroom was set off to one side of the department. Three-quarters of the way there, she passed the second entrance to the kitchen that gave the staff closer access to the food supplies. The place was even noisier than usual, raised voices hashing over the startling news adding to the normal din of banging pots and slamming refrigerator doors and the hum of the dishwasher. Pippa's stomach growled over the commotion.

Several more steps brought her to the storeroom. She unlatched the door and entered, pulling it closed firmly behind her. She'd been warned that leaving the door open could prove potentially hazardous to those exiting the kitchen with their hands full.

Grateful for the easy task Connie had assigned her, Pippa nevertheless had a difficult time concentrating. Rather than being focused on canned goods and spices, her mind was split between Lamont and her cosuspect in crime. If the truth be known, she'd rather think about Sky Thornton than a dead man—no contest there.

If only she could figure out what he wanted from her.

Could be she was reading warning signs that didn't exist. Could be she was too intrigued to trust him. She hadn't been attracted to a man since Dutch. Could be that because her late husband had not only treated her with disrespect but had been faithless, as well, she would judge all men against him, much to their detriment, at least for some time. Hadn't she thought Sky reminded her of someone?

She'd probably been imagining things, looking for a reason to distrust him. She wasn't in any sort of psychological state to be getting involved with a man. Her emotions were still a mess. She didn't trust her own instincts anymore.

To add to the confusion, her life was still very much in transition. She was trying to figure out where she fit into the scheme of things. Unfortunately, having worked in various departments of Westbrook's hadn't clarified the specifics of her future for her.

So, until she got her own life straightened out, she certainly couldn't get involved in someone else's—not even if that someone was tall and handsome with gorgeous blue eyes and the body of an athlete. . . .

A rasping noise outside the door jarred Pippa back to reality. Heart fluttering, she gasped. Praying that it wasn't Connie returning from her meeting so soon, she set to her task with determination. She had no intention of being caught mooning about instead of working. That she was the boss didn't seem to matter as much as her earning the respect of the people employed by Westbrook's.

Having finished a few minutes later, she made her way through the maze of metal shelving to the door . . .

. . . *which wouldn't open.*

At first she figured the thing was stuck and tried to shoulder it while jiggling the knob, but the solid wooden panel refused to budge. Had someone accidentally thrown the latch? Undoubtedly that was the noise that had startled her out of her reverie a few minutes before.

Resigned, she thumped on the panel. "Someone, open the door." More thumping. "It's Pippa. I'm locked in the storeroom."

Pressing her ear to the wood, she listened for a response, perhaps footsteps, only then realizing how thick and solid the old door was. Noises coming from the kitchen were faint, sounding farther away than she knew them to be. No doubt the workers couldn't even hear her.

"Hey, open up!" she yelled, banging hard on the door. "I'm in the storeroom!"

Still no response that she could tell. Really great! She could scream herself hoarse and not be heard over the din in the kitchen. She set her clipboard down on some nearby shelving. Who the heck had latched the door, anyway?

Aggravated, she tried again…and again…*and again.*
"I don't believe this!"

If anyone heard, they were ignoring her. She was beginning to feel uneasy. It was halfway through the afternoon. What if everyone went home without figuring out why she was missing? Or even that she *was* missing. Even Connie might not be suspicious, considering she hadn't even shown up that morning. The manager might merely think Pippa had been called away to another session with the police. She could be stuck here all night.

That notion made her nervous. Though she wasn't exactly claustrophobic, the idea of being left alone in a tiny storeroom until morning wouldn't thrill anyone. Gooseflesh cakewalked up her spine, and adrenaline lit her arteries with a thousand watts.

Energy renewed, Pippa yelled and beat on the door until her throat and fists were sore. Now what? She looked around at the steel shelving for some kind of tool. Getting creative, she picked up a large can of artichoke hearts and, holding it between both hands, began hammering the heavy metal container against the thick wood.

So engrossed was she in her attack on the door, that when it suddenly flew open, she went flying, too...

"Omigod!"

...slamming Sky Thornton to the floor. Only luck and a quick duck saved the naturalist from a collision with the artichoke can.

Pippa gasped. Pulse racing, she was pressed against Sky's length in a suggestive manner. Breast to chest. Hip to hip. Thighs tangled with thighs.

Not that he was complaining.

"What are *you* doing here?" she demanded, squirming—trying to get away.

Large hands firmly anchored around her waist, he wouldn't let her. "Looking for you."

She pushed at his chest—solid and warm beneath her palms. She was panting. *From the effort.* Certainly not from being trapped cheek to jowl with an attractive man.

"What's going on?" came a voice from the kitchen.

The next thing Pippa knew, a half-dozen workers were crowding the doorway, gaping. To top it off, Connie returned to the department in time to witness the debacle. Openmouthed, the manager immediately raced down the hall. Giving Sky a filthy look that finally persuaded him to let go of her, a highly embarrassed Pippa untangled herself and quickly got to her feet, while Sky took his time.

"I was locked in the storeroom," Pippa complained, relieved to be free, yet unable to still her racing pulse. She avoided looking directly at the man who'd cushioned her fall. He was standing close—too close. "I've been trying to get someone's attention for several minutes!"

"Who would have latched the door without checking the storeroom first?" Connie asked, in a voice reflecting her irritation. She faced her staff. "Well?"

"I didn't do it."

"I haven't left the kitchen."

"Don't look at me."

So it was unanimous. No one had thrown the bolt. "It just latched all by itself, right?" Pippa asked sarcastically. Maybe someone was trying to play a joke on her. "Okay, so is this my initiation into the Solemn Order of Caterers?" But her half-forced smile slipped when the collective response was a set of blank stares.

Shrugging, unable to accept that someone disliked her enough to try to scare her, Pippa chose to believe she'd had some kind of freak experience.

"You should get rid of that bolt," Sky growled.

"It's there because the door has a tendency to pop open from the vibration of the subway trains." The rapid transit system lay directly under the store. "That can be a hazard to someone who has hands full."

"So replace the bolt with a lock and key."

Ignoring him, Pippa reached inside the storeroom and retrieved the clipboard, which she then handed to

Connie. Only at that moment did she realize the manager wasn't carrying the pad of lined paper she'd left with. "All ingredients accounted for." And though it was some time before quitting, Pippa chose to exercise her executive privilege. "I have a meeting myself," she fibbed.

Connie gave Sky one of her looks. "I see."

"This is Sky Thornton, the man who was driving the sleigh Saturday night."

A buzz spread among the workers. Disregarding it— and Sky—Pippa set off down the hall, removing the apron she hadn't needed after all. The man followed so close on her heels, she could practically feel his breath on her neck. Well, not exactly. He was so tall he'd have to be stooping to get anywhere near her neck. But she experienced the sensation, anyway.

"So how long is this meeting going to take?"

"What makes you think it's any of your business?" she asked, noticing the pad of lined paper on the desk.

The same pad Connie had left with, though the top page was still blank. And it hadn't been in the manager's hand when she'd walked into the department, which prompted Pippa to think Connie had returned earlier....

"I was merely curious as to when you would be free," Sky pressed, forcing her attention on him.

"For what?"

"We need to talk."

"Been there. Done that."

About to reach for her suit jacket, she realized that, rather than hanging from its hook, the garment was lumped on the floor below. Frowning, she stooped to retrieve it, then dusted off the soiled material.

"We've only just begun," Sky was saying.

"Isn't that a song?" she asked, distracted.

Was this a weird happening, too, or had someone been messing with her jacket? And why?

"Tonight," Sky insisted.

"Tonight's the wake."

"Good enough."

About to slip into the garment, Pippa noticed the edge of the pocket was torn away a bit from the front panel. She was certain the pocket had been solidly sewn on when she'd thrown the film to the back of her desk drawer.

The film.

Had someone locked the door on her before searching her jacket for it? Then the happening might not have been so weird, after all.

Sky had seen the roll of film in her hand . . . and he'd seen her slip it into the jacket pocket. Giving him a thoughtful look, she reluctantly agreed. "Tonight, after the wake."

How else would she get to the truth about Sky Thornton?

And on the odd chance she couldn't . . . Pippa determined to get the film processed as quickly as possible in hopes that the prints might reveal some of the puzzling man's secrets.

SECRETS. WHO WOULD EVER figure she had any? Gwen Walsh thought as she paced the reception area. And if she was very, very clever, no one ever would.

About to ask the receptionist if Rand might be free soon, she was relieved when an elevator deposited his sister, Pippa, a few yards away.

In turn seeming distracted then surprised, Pippa acknowledged her. "Gwen. Did we have a meeting?"

Though having the fund-raiser at the store had been Lamont's idea, Pippa had actually done quite a bit of the planning for the event with Gwen, especially the catering and decoration.

"No, no meeting," she said. "I just dropped by to pick up some things . . . from Lamont's office."

"What things?"

"Coalition business. I need to find a new legal counsel as quickly as possible." Gwen felt her pulse race as she waited for the other woman's reaction. "Whoever I choose will want access to all our records immediately."

"Of course. Is someone getting them for you?"

"No. Actually, I was waiting to see your brother. He's been tied up since I got here." She sighed, hoping she sounded like the saint of patience. "I guess waiting a bit longer won't hurt."

Pippa shook her head. "No reason you should have to wait another minute." And she began to head straight for the lawyer's office. "C'mon. I can get the records for you."

"Great."

As she followed the redhead, Gwen smiled with genuine satisfaction. Though only a few years younger than she, Pippa was a bit naive, certainly not the brightest of the McNabbs. She would never suspect a thing.

But Gwen's optimistic perspective hit the skids after she took the thick file folders that Pippa pulled from the cabinet located directly behind Lamont's desk. She quickly reviewed their contents. While several were filled with legal documents, the one she was most anxious to get her hands on wasn't among them.

"Is this everything?" she asked, hoping her rising anxiety didn't creep into the simple question.

Pippa reopened the file drawer and made a quick reassessment. "That's it. Everything else here pertains to Westbrook's."

Before the other woman could question her, Gwen shrugged and forced a lie to her lips. "Just double-checking."

Unfortunately, she would have to keep on checking—and do whatever else it took to find the document that could implicate her in Lamont Birch's murder.

Chapter Five

A murder certainly called for a grandiose wake, Sky thought upon arriving at the Silent Night Funeral Home, though he was too cynical to believe Lamont Birch had charmed this many people into caring for him. Many of the supposed mourners were here because it was the politically correct thing to do, part of the price of doing business. Others were seeking publicity from the reporters who worked the crowd.

The rear of the salon was packed near to bursting, people spilling out into the hall and gathering in small knots, where they conversed as if they didn't have a care in the world. At the front of the salon, the pewter coffin itself stood a lonely sentinel—mournerless—surrounded only by wreaths and bouquets reflecting both the solemn occasion and the holiday season.

Drawing closer, Sky scanned the room as if he could recognize guilt when he saw it. At least one person had hated Lamont Birch, and he figured a murderer probably had enough guts to show at the wake—undoubtedly one of those men or women avoiding getting an up-close-and-personal gander at the dead man.

"I'm so sorry, Acacia, darling," a woman was saying to the lawyer's dry-eyed widow, who held court a good distance from the dais. "Let us know if there's anything we can do."

"Thank you, Sophie," Acacia calmly answered, touching cheeks with the woman in the silver fox. "You and Jonathan were very dear to Lamont."

Acacia Birch was dressed in black. At least the color was appropriate, even if the provocative cut of the garment was a bit unseemly for a wake. Acacia was dramatically ensconced among the largest and most brilliant red poinsettias he'd ever seen.

How festive.

Eyes narrowing, Sky tore his gaze from the widow with too little grief to spare for the husband she was about to bury. Inching through the crowd toward the coffin, he searched the room for Pippa.

"Sky, there you are."

He stopped and turned toward the familiar voice belonging to Valerie Quinlan. "Evening." Casting a glance behind the mayor's aide, he added, "You're here without His Honor?"

"Mayor Keegan will be arriving any moment."

"So you're the front guard, waiting to announce his big entrance."

"I'm here to pay my respects, because I'm sorry a man is dead."

Now why did he have trouble believing her? Maybe because she'd zeroed in on him, rather than taking that stroll straight to the coffin. Choosing to force the issue, with instinct making him want to see her reaction when she did face the corpse, he took her elbow. Ushering her forward, he murmured, "Then by all means, let's pay our respects together."

Her arm stiffened under his hand. Her feet dragged. He glanced at Valerie as she hid what he could only describe as panic. He hadn't seriously thought of her as a suspect in Lamont's death, but her resistance was weird.

"Something wrong?"

"No, of course not. I've never been comfortable with—"

"Dead bodies?" he finished for her.

She didn't correct him, which made Sky wonder if there was reason to distrust the attractive blonde... or the man she worked for. Mayor Darby Keegan had been responsible for Sky's commitment to the fund-raiser, and therefore was responsible for Sky's being suspect. But had Keegan inadvertently involved Sky? Or had he planned it?

Christmas was supposed to be a time to celebrate a heavenly birth, not an earthly death. Sky recognized the irony as he moved Valerie closer to the coffin—although another person beat them to it.

Wearing a badly cut suit, the man was of less than average height, had a narrow back and thinning hair. He peered down at Birch closely, as if to prove to himself that the lawyer was indeed a corpse. Then he checked his watch, clucked and scurried back toward the exit as if he were late for a more important appointment. Sky watched the odd fellow until he was swallowed up by the crowd.

Another fast look for Pippa only frustrated him. He was beginning to wonder if she'd changed her mind about coming at all. Had he scared her off? The thought that he could affect her one way or the other gave him a certain satisfaction, though putting her off wouldn't suit his plans.

Turning back to Valerie, he realized she was standing frozen before the coffin. Her eyes were wide and red, as if she was about to burst into tears. She looked exactly as she had when he'd spotted her standing alone out on State Street that fatal night.

"You're certain nothing is wrong?"

"Of course something is wrong," she croaked, seeming to have difficulty swallowing. "A man I knew is dead, for God's sake."

Sky was confused by the conflicting remorse and fury that briefly crossed her features before she ducked her head and stalked away. He followed, wondering about the intensity of her reaction.

But the strength of any emotion was fleeting, and a moment later, she was calm. "Why don't we find where they're hiding the coffee."

Suspicions aroused again by her flirtatious tone— maybe he ought to credit her with superior acting skills—Sky flatly said, "I don't get it."

"What?"

"Exactly. What is it you want with me?"

"Having a cup of coffee together doesn't mean I want something from you."

Aware that his direct approach was renewing her jitters, he asked, "Doesn't it? Why did you choose to talk to me, rather than, say, the widow?"

"You're better-looking." Her joking tone was laced with tension.

"And you're not interested in paying your respects." He was observant enough to tell the difference. "So what gives?"

Valerie backed down. "All right. So maybe I'm not very good at playing private detective," she said flatly. "I'm just trying to score a few points with the boss. Mayor Keegan asked me to keep an eye on you tonight if you showed."

"Why?"

"I guess he thinks you might really have run Lamont over on purpose and—"

"And what if I did? That would make me a murderer." In a soft and menacing voice, he suggested, "Then you might be putting yourself in danger. Isn't that carrying loyalty a bit far?"

To his puzzlement, Valerie's expression lightened considerably, and she laughed in his face. "I know damn well that *you're* not the murderer. But keeping the mayor happy is my job."

There was no way Valerie Quinlan could know he wasn't a murderer...unless she knew *who was.* Herself, perhaps?

Not that Sky figured he was going to get it out of her. At least not without something more to go on, something he could use as leverage. But before he could begin a fishing expedition, a flurry of activity at the salon's door turned every head in the room, including his.

"There's the boss now," Valerie said, immediately leaving Sky's side to join the politician.

"'Tis a sad, sad day for the city of Chicago," Mayor Darby Keegan boomed in a pseudo-Irish accent, "when a respected, upstanding citizen like Lamont Birch isn't safe from a wretched murderer!"

His expression properly remorseful, the mayor posed quite nicely for several photographers before sweeping through the crowd, entourage following, stopping only when he reached the coffin. Having heard Keegan and Birch didn't get along—hated each other, as a matter of fact—Sky watched closely as the mayor made a pretense of saying his last goodbye to a dear old friend.

"There is none so well remembered as them that go before their time," the mayor pronounced with a perfectly straight face as he gazed down at the man who had insulted him with what had proved to be his last breath. "Lamont Birch, you will be remembered... and your death will be avenged!"

Sky was so involved in the ludicrous minidrama, that he was startled by a disgusted-sounding voice behind him. "Dear Lord, does he have to turn everything into a circus?"

Chest tightening oddly, Sky spun around to face Pippa McNabb. Even in a muted olive green dress, she shone. Her flawless complexion, emerald eyes and bright red hair set her apart from every other woman in the room. He hated that he noticed.

Forcing himself to glower at her, he said, "Sneaking up on a man could be dangerous."

She stared at him steadily, neither intimidated nor amused. "As could playing games with a woman."

The touch of innocence that normally softened her features was, for the moment, gone. Tempted to demand an explanation, Sky bit his tongue.

Playing games.

Surely she couldn't know who he was. But the way she was eyeing him—as if he were poison—he wondered. And despite all logic, he cared.

No good deed goes unpunished. Wasn't that a famous line from something? He wished he'd considered that possibility before giving in to the oft-repeated plea that he get closer to Pippa McNabb.

He'd gone against the grain and had gotten involved, and why? So he could prove something to himself after all these years? Look where his promise to dig up the truth about Pippa had landed him so far. The possibility of his getting intimately acquainted with a jail cell was not the kind of surprise he'd hoped to find in his Christmas stocking . . . no more than was an unwelcome emotional attachment to a woman he didn't even know and certainly shouldn't like.

Thinking he should stop now while he was ahead, walk away from this woman and keep a low profile until the police sorted it all out, Sky couldn't keep himself from egging Pippa on. "So who twisted your panty hose into a knot?"

Her soft jaw tightened. "Who said anyone did?"

"You look a little like an ogre." Once again he gave in to temptation and ran his thumb over her cheek. "Right here."

She flushed but held her ground. "Should I be jocular? Like the mayor, perhaps?"

"Please. Spare me."

"Then what is it you want from me?"

Again Sky had the feeling she was on to him. "Cooperation," he said, quickly trying to smooth things over.

"In what?"

A quick glance around assured him no one was tuning in to their conversation. Still, not wanting to chance the possibility, he steered her toward a quiet corner of the room. "In figuring out who was trying to set us up for Lamont Birch's murder."

Though he thought she might deny it, she finally said, "As if we could."

"Why not? You knew him."

"Not well—"

"Well enough," he insisted. "Can you honestly tell me you don't have some thoughts regarding who might have done him in?"

"I don't have a clue. I can't imagine anyone I know going around planning someone else's death."

Thrown for a moment, Sky stared. Was she for real? She sounded like a complete innocent. But how could she be, since this wasn't the first murder case she'd been involved in?

"I mean, I know it happens," she went on, her features reflecting inner pain. "By now, you've probably heard about the way my husband, Dutch, died. But he did things that weren't right. Pushed people too far. Not that I thought he should die for his sins," she quickly added.

Sky swallowed his own pain. "Someone did. And someone thought Lamont Birch should die, too. I propose we find out why, and maybe that will give us the who. We probably have a better chance at discovering his *sins* than the authorities."

The way she was looking at him was curious, as if she were trying to figure him out. "I'll think about it."

"Don't take too long."

The longer it took, the more time the murderer would have to cover his or her tracks. Sky was not about to take the fall for someone else. And though he'd been led to believe Pippa was out only for herself, he was beginning to doubt that in a big way. Working together, they could not only clear their names, but he could also make up his own mind about the woman about whom he was beginning to obsess.

Obsessed with presenting the facade of a properly grieving widow, Acacia Birch tried not to show her surprise as the two murder suspects approached her together, both wearing determined expressions. What in the world did they want with her? She sniffed at her onion-scented handkerchief so that tears sprang to her eyes.

Upon connecting gazes, Pippa appeared stricken. "I'm so sorry, Acacia."

She eyed the hand Pippa held out to her and wondered if it would be more prudent to take it or to refuse. Pippa *was* a suspect, after all. She compromised, hesitating a moment, then giving the younger woman a wilted hand, which she quickly withdrew. "Pippa." Even while acknowledging her, she looked past the red curls, searching for a familiar face—one she *wanted* to see.

"Acacia, would you mind telling me something?"

Making the effort to hide her growing displeasure, Acacia snapped her attention back to the chit, who was giving her the oddest stare. "Yes, dear, what is it?" She ignored the chill slipping up her spine.

"Exactly what was Lamont allergic to?"

Acacia's heart raced. "I beg your pardon?"

"Let's not pretend here." Pippa's gaze momentarily flicked away. "I most likely served him the food that killed him, yet I don't even know what that might be."

"Her knowing is only fair, isn't it?"

The sleigh driver—Acacia remembered his name was Schuyler Thornton because it had sounded so familiar—backed Pippa up.

Acacia took a deep breath and swallowed hard, as if this was something difficult for her to discuss. "Lamont had many allergies, the severe food allergies being watermelon, peanuts and shellfish, most notably shrimp." Tensely, she watched the twit wither before her.

"Shrimp on toast triangles." Pippa glanced at her companion. "One of the appetizers I served."

"Like you said, you didn't know," he reassured her. "And even though it's hard to mistake a shrimp for anything else, he obviously didn't notice."

"A terrible accident." Acacia left just the right note of doubt in her tone to discomfit the other woman. Anything to shake Pippa up so that she wouldn't be tempted to pry further. Bad enough the police had pestered her nearly beyond endurance. "You needn't upset yourself."

Acacia herself was not in the least upset, of course, though it would be wiser for her to fake a little more spousal loyalty than she'd been able to muster so far. She could do it. She only had this evening and the funeral the next morning to get through, after all. Drawing on her resources, she conjured up a broken sob. Pippa and her companion exchanged glances.

Indeed, Acacia decided, adding an effective sniff, it would be best if no one guessed exactly how glad she was that Lamont was out of her life for good.

"I SORT OF GET the feeling Acacia Birch is not exactly devastated," Pippa whispered to Sky once they'd left her to other people.

"She does seem to be embracing widowhood in stride."

Not wanting to believe anything really bad about the woman—not even that she'd actually been faking her grief—Pippa gave Acacia the benefit of the doubt. "She could be in shock."

"Or she could have had reasons to want her husband dead."

Pippa chewed on that for a moment. Acacia Birch a suspect? Though she'd never been fond of the society woman, she could hardly imagine her killing anyone.

Still…she hadn't forgotten how composed Acacia had been on the night of the tragedy. "I suppose there could be reasons," she admitted reluctantly.

"Like money."

"Uh-uh. You're way off base there."

"Aren't we being a bit naive?"

Pippa snorted at his supercilious attitude. "Acacia Birch has more money than she knows what to do with. Well, certainly more than Lamont ever had. She grew up on a ten-acre estate in Winnetka, the only child of elderly parents. Her father ran his own company. Acacia inherited everything." Even though she hadn't known the couple well, the information was common knowledge around the store. "Lamont didn't grow up poor or anything, and he made quite a bit as a lawyer, but I'll bet his assets were a fraction of hers."

"Maybe we can find something in *that* if we put our heads together long enough."

"We? I don't remember agreeing to a partnership." Though the way his crowding her made her uncomfortable—instinct warning her to run as fast as she could— Pippa suspected that if she was around Sky Thornton long enough, he probably could get her to sign a blank check. Flushing, she gritted her teeth and added, "I said I'd think about it."

"Think about what?" Joining them, Rand slipped an arm around her waist and kissed her cheek.

Sky said, "I want your sister to—"

"Go out for something to eat," Pippa said, cutting him off. She gave Sky a warning look not to say anything further. In turn, his dark eyebrows shot up and his blue eyes glittered with amusement.

"I thought you were going out with Shelby and me," Rand complained.

"I am."

"But you just told the man you'd think about it."

"You did," Sky said, his sudden grin perverse. "But I'm willing to make it tomorrow night."

She was trapped and by her own big mouth. "All right." Trying not to show her irritation, she agreed, "Tomorrow night."

"I'll be looking forward to it."

"There's Shelby waiting for us over by the door now," Rand said. " 'Night, Thornton."

"McNabb."

As Rand whisked her away, Pippa was certain she heard Sky's soft laughter trail after her. But when she turned to glare in his direction, he had once again vanished into the crowd.

She determined to put him out of mind.

PIPPA COULD BARELY EAT a bite with Rand and Shelby. Her appetite seemed to have vanished, so Pippa chose to leave and caught a taxi rather than pull them away from their dinners. On the ride to her Hawthorn Street address, Sky and his proposition were again uppermost in her mind. For once, wanting to make a decision for herself, she hadn't mentioned the possibility of playing detective with the stranger to her brother. No doubt Rand would freak out at the merest whisper of danger where she was concerned.

Though how dangerous could it be to make a few inquiries of her own? She'd already called Pop for a copy of the autopsy report and had delivered the film to one of those twenty-four-hour places.

"Here we are, miss, safe and sound," the gruff old driver said over the squeal of his brakes. He glanced out at the stately old home located on a large double lot less than a block west of Lake Shore Drive, the freeway separating high rises from Lincoln Park and Lake Michigan. "You got lights on. Good. Someone's waiting for you."

How nice that he sounded like he cared. Though the fare was barely ten dollars, Pippa handed the man a twenty and said, "Keep the change. Merry Christmas."

"Hey, thanks. Happy holidays to you, too!"

Sliding out of the taxi, Pippa only wished she had something to celebrate—and someone to celebrate with.

A fine layer of snow crunched beneath her feet as she made her way up the walk. Behind her, the taxi chugged away. She stopped. Listened to the quiet. It was too cold for people to be wandering about. The neighborhood seemed deserted but for the lights in the nearby buildings. Her breath whitened the air before her. Above, as if waiting for the chance to dump another load on the unwary, snow clouds hung low and foreboding. No stars decorating the heavens tonight.

For a moment, she imagined a drift of white curling from one of her chimneys. But that, of course, was impossible. Only ghosts waited for her inside—ghosts and crimson memories.

Once a week, she had a woman in to clean and a man to do the yard work and heavy lifting. She lived alone. Contrary to the taxi driver's assumption, no one was waiting for her. Automatic timers had lit the house room by room shortly after dark.

The beautiful old place sparkled with holiday cheer. Garlands of greenery caught up with red ribbon decorated the rail of the porch that ran halfway around the gray-sided building. The stained-and-leaded-glass insets in the windows and door that were original to the house were surrounded with tiny Christmas lights. They, along with the surfeit of warm carved woods and ceramic fireplaces, gave the place a character that had been impossible to part with after Dutch's death.

About to go inside, Pippa hesitated when she heard a noise out back. A frisson of unease beset her, yet she shook it away.

Winter brought animals to her backyard on a daily basis—cold and hungry stray cats and dogs, in addition to the squirrels and birds that normally inhabited the tiny wooded area in back of the house. She hated for anyone—even a small animal—to go away hungry.

Hearing the soft noise again, she moved toward it, past several deciduous trees, whose barren branches reached up to the sky in supplication as if begging for protection from the gazebo crouched in the back, a menacing dark silhouette against the snow. Startled by her own imagination, Pippa wondered what she was thinking. Trees were trees, and she'd turned the gazebo into a makeshift shelter using plastic panels as windbreaks and setting thick, fuzzy pads on the benches that lined the small building. Nothing ominous there. She was merely jumpy.

Thinking that hearing her own voice would settle her down, she called, "Hey, who's there?" She kept her words soft so as not to scare the animal off. "Kitty? Doggy?"

No answering meow or bark. She made a sharp *tch-tch-tch* sound, which the squirrels liked, though she rarely saw one of the little rodents after dark. No answer. No skittering noise. Nothing. She slowed her steps. An arctic gust of wind made the house's windows rattle and her teeth chatter. And despite the fact that the walk had been shoveled the day before, icy snow spilled into her shoes.

Pippa shivered. And listened. And watched. Or tried to. For some reason, the back was awfully dark, with only a bit of light from the alley spilling through tree branches to the grounds. The porch light must have burned out.

Big deal.

So why was she so hesitant to continue?

She held her breath until she heard another noise— this one from the garbage cans in the alley. Tension drained from her body, leaving her limp and feeling a bit foolish. She'd scared the animal, after all, and it had gotten away.

But since she was already back here, she might as well set out some of the feed she kept secreted in an alcove under the gazebo. Not having had time to give the animals she regularly fed a thought since the tragedy, Pippa didn't want them to feel abandoned. If they didn't venture out for food now, they certainly would first thing in the morning.

To that end, she dug in her coat pocket for her key ring. Using the attached small flashlight, she raided the winter larder, setting out ears of corn on stakes for the squirrels, filling feeders with seed for the birds and pouring dog food into one big bowl, cat food into another, and leaving them at opposite doorways to the gazebo. No need to bother with setting out water that would only freeze during the night. Enough snow lay on the ground that the animals wouldn't go thirsty, and she could see to fresh water in the morning.

Satisfied with her positive efforts, feeling enormously better than she had all day, Pippa closed up the animal pantry. About to retrace her steps, she decided to take care of the burned-out light, as well. Illuminating the path with her thin flashlight beam, she made her way to the back steps. It wasn't until she was on the landing that she realized not only was the porch light out, but the kitchen was also oddly dark.

Could the timer have broken?

Reaching for the back door, she hesitated a second too long.

Footsteps behind Pippa alerted her, but too late. Heart thumping, pulse racing, she'd barely started to turn when something hard and unforgiving crashed down on the base of her skull.

Pippa saw twinkling stars, after all...and then nothing.

Chapter Six

"Pippa, wake up. Pippa, say something, please."

The unconscious woman cradled in Sky's arms stirred. The sound issuing from her lips progressed from a low moan to an elongated groan of pain. His eyes having adjusted to the dark, he could barely make out her face. Her lashes were fluttering, as if she was doing her best to obey.

"That's it," he urged. "C'mon. We've got to get you inside."

He was ready to scoop her up in his arms and break through the back door. Before he could move, her eyes flashed open and she weakly pushed against him. "No... get away from me!"

"Hey, calm down." It didn't take a genius to figure out she was panicked and not thinking straight. Sky forced himself to say, "*I'm* not the one who laid you out," despite the invisible fist that suddenly closed around his chest, making him realize that deep inside, he really didn't want her to be afraid of him.

Though she stopped struggling, she kept her hands clawed between them as if ready to strike out. "Why should I believe you?"

He tried logic. "If I'd done this to you, why would I still be here?"

Tension gradually oozed out of Pippa, and for a moment, she lay motionless in his arms, as limp as a rag doll. "There's some logic in that, I suppose. Must have been a mugger who assumed I was carrying a purse." She patted the side of her coat. "Wallet's still here." Then she was struggling again, this time to rise.

"Hold on," Sky ordered, stretching an arm across her back and hooking his hand around her waist. "Let me help you." She felt so good pressed against him, he didn't want to let her go. But once he got her to her feet, he did exactly that. "Christmas is the season for robberies. The nicer the house, the more inviting a target."

"How did you find me?" she asked abruptly.

"I was on the front porch, ready to ring the doorbell, when I heard a scuffle back here . . . and a thump that was obviously you going down for the count. I came running and your attacker made a quick getaway through the alley."

"What did he look like?"

"Sorry. All I saw was a dark streak. I was more concerned with you."

He'd acted on instinct rather than logic in rushing to her—he'd known it was Pippa before he'd gotten close enough to see her. Had he first gotten a better look at the assailant running away, he could have given the police a description. She was thoughtful for a moment before asking, "How did you know where I lived?"

And Sky drew on the evasiveness he'd learned to cultivate long ago when he'd first chosen to remain anonymous. "In my line of work, you learn to be resourceful."

Her hand shook as she tried to use the keys on the back door. He took the ring from her, then noticed the hole punched in one of the door's glass panels—courtesy of her burglar. She must have foiled the attempt at a break-in. The knob gave easily under his hand.

Once in the kitchen, she flipped on the ceiling light. "You can leave now."

"You're welcome, I'm sure, but I'm not going anywhere."

He locked the back door behind him and made a mental note to take care of the break in the glass later. He'd find a piece of plywood or something and block the hole. The lock itself looked as old as the door. Hadn't she ever heard of modern dead bolts?

Rather than pressing her about precautions now, he simply said, "You may not be safe. Besides, I really should get you to an emergency room."

"No hospital!"

"Then I'll call your—"

"No doctor, either. Or family," she quickly interrupted. "I'll be fine."

But she wasn't fine. Swaying on her feet, she needed his support to get to the front of the house and his help in removing her coat and gloves. The thin leather had barely protected her hands, which felt like blocks of ice. He rubbed at them and attempted to ignore his growing awareness of her as a desirable woman. "Good thing I know first aid," he growled testily when she pulled a hand free.

His gaze met hers and he was stirred despite himself. Something about Pippa got to him in a big way. She was turning out to be contrary to everything he'd been led to expect. Forcing away the unwelcome thought that stirred a bit of guilt in him, he deposited her on an overstuffed cream-colored sofa in front of the fire-place, where logs had burned down to embers. About that, he couldn't help lecturing her.

"You should never go off leaving a fire burning, you know. Not if you want to make certain your house is still standing when you come home."

"I didn't..." Her words drifted off and her eyes widened as they connected with the embers. She flashed him a look, then winced at the quick movement.

"You didn't what?"

"The last fire I built was Friday night," she insisted.

"Your housekeeper, maybe?"

"Today wasn't her day to clean. Do you think a bur-glar would have the audacity...?" Her eyes grew even wider and she gulped.

Sky followed her gaze to an empty glass and a half-eaten plate of cookies on an end table near the hearth. "What?"

Groaning, she sank back into the cushions and mumbled, "Maybe I'm dreaming. More like having a nightmare. Between breaking into my house and knocking me out, the culprit built a fire and had a snack!"

He had to admit that was pretty weird. But as much as he might like to figure out motives, he was more concerned with making certain she was all right. He checked her eyes. No concussion. Her pulse—a bit thready. Her head—a little lump but no bleeding.

"You'll live," he solemnly pronounced.

Pippa winced as she rested the back of her head against the sofa. "Must I?" She shuddered suddenly and clasped her arms around herself.

Sky figured the room was warm enough. Determin-ing that her nerves needed steadying, he found her liquor cabinet and splashed a little brandy into a glass. "Take it slow. Roll it around in your mouth and let it drizzle down your throat." When she hesitated, he assured her, "You're suffering from shock. A small amount of alcohol will make you feel better."

After she took the glass and sipped at the brandy, Sky began busying himself with a safety check. He made certain all the downstairs windows were locked, as well as the two additional doors, neither of which had a modern dead bolt.

"Living alone as you do in the heart of a big city, why in the world don't you have better security?" he demanded to know.

"I never felt like I wanted to live in a prison."

"Some precautions only make sense. Those locks are antiquated. Your doors all have glass insets. The least you could do is install dead bolts that are secured with a key from the inside as well as the outside. Wrought-iron gratings over the glass wouldn't be out of order, either."

"You're probably right."

He couldn't believe she wasn't arguing with him. As a matter of fact, she seemed practically oblivious. Her attention was focused on the Christmas tree that graced the nook near the front hall.

"What now?" he asked.

"The Christmas presents. They're all still under the tree. Undisturbed."

Indeed, more than a dozen fancily wrapped packages lay beneath the pine branches. "So? What's your point?"

"If the person who broke in here was a common thief, why didn't he take them? Or at least open the packaging to see what was inside?" Her gaze flashed toward the dining room. "And what about the silver?"

Various perfectly polished serving pieces sat in full view on the breakfront. As far as Sky could tell, they hadn't even been touched. Nothing seemed to have been disturbed anywhere, and there were many quietly expensive items of porcelain and several modest sculptures dotting nooks and crannies in the dining and living rooms.

Sky was getting a bad feeling about this. "If not a burglar, then who?"

Her features transformed her from a slightly upset young woman to one who was very much afraid. Of what? Or who? What secret was *she* hiding?

Must be something to do with Lamont Birch's death, and if so, then he should know about it. Not that he expected her to tell without some convincing... He could do it, though, if he put his mind to the task. And why shouldn't he?

Coiled on the couch, Pippa appeared so vulnerable. Maybe that's why he hesitated. The softer side of Sky wanted to curl up next to her. To take her in his arms. To make her feel safe rather than hassle her.

Trouble was, she wasn't safe from him. And eventually, she would learn his identity and realize what he wanted with her. Then she would no doubt hate him. Not that he should care...

He would never complete his mission if he let conflicting feelings get in the way. And then he would never know the truth. He needed to get close to Pippa McNabb, but if he started caring about her too much— about her emotions—he would be in trouble.

Big time!

MORE TROUBLE. The fiasco with the McNabb woman should never have happened.

Headlights off, the car crawled to a stop in front of the house, where the driver snugged it close to a larger Thunderbird for camouflage. Parking in this over-crowded city neighborhood was a matter of luck, any-way. Good thing there were alleys where a vehicle could be left long enough to do a job.

But thinking about the forced run to the car several minutes before, the driver groaned. How could this night's work have gone so wrong?

Pippa McNabb was supposed to have been having dinner with her brother and sister-in-law. That should have taken a couple of hours. Instead she'd sneaked home early and ruined everything. Well, maybe *every-thing* was somewhat an exaggeration. The first floor had gotten a quick once-over. If only there'd been time to search the rest of the place...and for a clean get-away, as well. At least nothing else had been left be-hind in the hurry to get out. No clues to set anyone's suspicions cooking.

A sharp scrutiny through the big bay window proved to be enlightening. Even from the distance of the street, Schuyler Thornton was visible pacing the room. He'd obviously been the one to come to her rescue. So the two had joined forces—undoubtedly the reason she'd returned early.

The driver tightened gloved fingers around the steer-ing wheel. Thornton's getting involved didn't bode well for the scheme already in motion. Too late to back out now. Besides which, too many people already held pieces of the puzzle. In time, someone was certain to put them together and reach some incriminating conclusions. And everyone knew two heads were better than one.

Going to jail again was out of the question . . . no matter what had to be done to prevent such a scenario. The very thought set off a flurry of unwelcome physical reactions. Pounding heart. Sweaty palms. Dry mouth. No, never again.

But maybe it wouldn't come to a question of incarceration. Maybe no one would find out until it was too late. It was likely Pippa had chalked up this particular incident to a holiday break-in. If she called the police, they would certainly steer her to that probability. If so, then for a while longer, the truth would be safely hidden. Hopefully, there would be enough opportunity to pull off the coup of the season and hide the tracks.

And if things were looking shaky, getting rid of anyone who presented a stumbling block—permanently, if necessary—would relegate another sentence in the state pen to nothing more than a distant crimson nightmare.

THE CRIMSON NIGHTMARE was becoming more vivid.

Someone breaking into her home . . . eating her Christmas cookies . . . drinking her milk . . .

Pippa would have laughed if the incident hadn't been so bizarrely frightening. Her head whirled and she laid it back against the couch and the ice pack Sky had made up for her.

"Better?" he asked, sounding gruff and trying not to appear overly concerned.

"Getting there."

"So why don't you want to call the police?"

"Nothing was stolen."

He stared at her hard as if looking through her eyes into her very soul. "But it might have been. And the thief could try again. Unless there's some other reason..."

She shifted uncomfortably and went with a half truth. "I'm wondering if this didn't have something to do with Lamont."

"How so?"

"I don't know," she hedged, for some reason choosing not to bring up the film. "I haven't exactly had time to think about it, have I?"

What if the thief had broken in to steal the roll, not realizing she'd already taken it in for processing? She flashed Sky a sharp look. Wondering. Had he wanted the film enough to break into her place, knock her over the head and then lie in an attempt to gain her confidence?

Her fingertips worked at the torn pocket of her jacket....

Then again, who was to say someone else hadn't witnessed her find, as well. The first floor of Westbrook's couldn't have been more public. Hundreds of people had been milling about. Still, she couldn't bring herself to chance mentioning it. Not yet. Not until she was sure of him. That meant seeing the photos. Alone.

"Maybe if we put our heads together, we can figure it out," Sky was saying as he paced between her and the fireplace, where the embers still glowed.

"Figure what out?"

"What the thief wanted, of course."

"Any suggestions?" Pippa asked.

"How well did you know Lamont Birch?"

"Now you're sounding like Lieutenant Jackson." His question annoyed her. "Not well."

"You knew enough about his finances."

Reminded of the information she'd shared about the Birches earlier, Pippa grew defensive. "Common knowledge."

"Hearsay?"

Thinking that now he sounded like a lawyer—like Lamont himself would if he were still alive—Pippa couldn't hold back her sarcastic tone. "I certainly never had a look at his bank books, if that's what you're getting at."

"What *did* you have a look at?"

Was he subtly referring to the film? Pippa chose to throw him off the track. Rising from the couch, she moved closer to the fireplace. A breath of warmth enveloped her. From the fire? Or from Sky as he brushed by her?

"Well, I'll have a look at the autopsy report tomorrow." She figured telling him that much wouldn't hurt anything after their conversation with Acacia. "I used my influence. I asked Pop to get it." Facing Sky directly, she stared at him hard. "Oh, I guess you don't know—Pop's a cop."

Though Pippa searched his expression for some sign of surprise at the information, he didn't even blink, making her certain that he *had* known. Just as he'd known who she was. And where she lived.

Before she could challenge him, he asked, "What do you hope to gain from seeing the report?"

"Actually, I wanted to know what Lamont was allergic to."

"Shrimp—courtesy of the widow. I thought we'd established that."

"True." Though when she tried to visualize Lamont putting that shrimp on a toast triangle in his mouth, she couldn't. Then again, she'd been too concerned with cooling his and the mayor's heated tempers to remember details. "But I already talked to Pop earlier. And you never know what Lieutenant Jackson *didn't* say. Maybe we'll find out something else."

Sky stopped in his tracks. "*We* will?" His thick eyebrows shot up. "Then you've thought about it? Decided you want to throw your lot in with me?"

"Cautiously."

Though she'd like to believe that having been mugged outside her own home was an occurrence unconnected to any other, she figured that was about as likely as Lamont inadvertently eating what was unmistakably shrimp, then accidentally falling in front of eight running reindeer, all within the same hour. She didn't have to be convinced that her attacker and the current Santa killer were one and the same. She just had to figure out why the murderer was after her.

Only the film came to mind.

Then to be perverse, knowing she shouldn't trust Sky Thornton any further than she could throw him, Pippa rationalized, telling herself that his showing up in time to rescue her twice—first from the storeroom, now from the attacker—*was* coincidence and that he meant her no harm. Though she was certain he wanted to find the real murderer for selfish reasons, she also wanted to believe Sky was equally concerned about her welfare.

But how concerned?

Surely Sky wasn't involving himself deeper in this murder mystery *for* her. Pippa was touched by the possibility, even as she mentally pushed him away, telling herself that he wouldn't be good for her, that if she were ready for a relationship, this time it would be with a man who didn't have an edge. With someone as different from Dutch as she could find.

"Well, that's certainly a switch," Sky was saying, shaking her loose from her private thoughts. "So it's to be you and me together."

The way he was looking at her now made her uncomfortable. As if he was referring to more than their working together. As if he'd read her very thoughts. He moved closer. She had nowhere to go but directly into the fire, so she stood her ground.

"Working together...so to speak," she agreed lightly, feeling the pulse pound in her throat. Her hand fluttered to her neck, as if she could hide her reaction from him. "Let's face it, we're rank amateurs. We don't really know how to go about this. We might drive ourselves nuts for nothing."

Like a loving caress, his gaze swept over the fingers protecting her pulse from him. "And we might save ourselves some grief."

She took a steadying breath. "You mean being arrested."

"Or worse."

Pippa knew he was referring to the attack. Suggesting there might be another and that next time she might not be so lucky. Shuddering, she wrapped her arms around her middle and turned away from him. Staring down into the gently glowing embers, she felt a stirring. She could feel warmth from both directions. All too aware of Sky behind her, she shifted restlessly until his hands encircled her shoulders.

Then she froze.

Heart pounding, mouth suddenly gone dry, she waited for his next move. Not knowing what she would do, how she would respond. Closing her eyes, she expected to envision Dutch's face wearing that loopy grin that had once attracted her to him. She didn't, though,

"Did you ever hear of knocking?" she asked. Pippa was immediately aware of her pulse surging, the fast-building exhilaration dispelling her depression. Sky's very presence animated her. When would she learn? Her mother had always bemoaned the fact that Pippa was attracted to men who wore an aura of power as easily as a second skin and predicted that she would live to regret it. Dutch certainly had proven her mother right.

Closing the door behind him, Sky said, "I figured you'd want to see me."

She did, God help her, not that she would say so. Instead she asked, "What's on your mind this morning?" and sat straighter in her chair.

"The autopsy report."

Pippa started. Good Lord, she'd forgotten all about it. Immediately scrabbling through the stacks on her desk, she found the envelope from a messenger service piled amid some other mail. "Here it is."

"So you haven't looked at it yet?"

"I haven't been here long. And I did have a few other things on my mind."

Like guilt.

She slit open the envelope that would confirm what until now had merely been a perception. Pulling out the multipage report, she reluctantly scanned the medical examiner's summary. "No new information here." Disappointing, but she hadn't really expected otherwise. "Just as Lieutenant Jackson stated, the medical examiner couldn't decide whether the anaphylactic shock or the accident was the true cause of death."

"What about the stomach contents?"

Despite the conclusions she'd drawn after her chat with Acacia, Pippa flipped through the report, found the correct page and scanned the list. Hardly able to breathe, she murmured, "That's weird."

"What?"

She met his intent gaze. "No shrimp."

"Let me see." Pippa handed Sky the report. Wedging a hip on the edge of her desk, he read aloud, "Turkey, chicken livers, bacon, cheese, apples, celery, peanuts, pineapple..." He paused and scanned the remaining items. "You're right. No shrimp."

Her heart thundered in her chest as she jumped out of the chair. "Lamont didn't eat any shrimp!" She rounded the desk and stopped next to Sky.

He turned back to the beginning of the report to peruse the medical examiner's summary. "Yet there's no doubt about the anaphylactic shock," he said. "What other food allergies did his widow mention? Watermelon, right?"

"Right." Pippa had been so convinced that the shrimp had done Lamont in, she hadn't thought about the other possibilities. "Watermelon, shellfish, especially shrimp...and peanuts!" She grabbed the sheets from Sky's hand and flipped back to the list. "Peanuts! They found peanuts in his stomach! Don't you see what that means?"

Sky shrugged. "That you pegged the wrong food as having done him in."

Never having felt such a deep sense of relief, Pippa picked up the telephone, saying, "We didn't serve anything made with peanuts that night. I didn't have anything to do with Lamont's death, not even by accident. I'm not guilty!" She started to dial. "But someone sure is!" Although once connected with Lieutenant Jackson, convincing the man that he should cross her off his list of suspects was another matter.

After she quickly explained the reason for her call, Jackson coolly said, "Thank you for telling me what I already know, Miss McNabb."

Sky was huddled with his head so close to hers that Pippa was certain he could hear everything. Physical awareness triggered, despite the seriousness of the situation, she tried not to let him distract her.

Jackson added, "I won't ask how you got your hands on confidential police records."

And she wasn't about to volunteer the information. "But this lets me off the hook, right?"

"Why should it?"

"Lamont Birch was allergic to peanuts." Pippa couldn't believe she had to spell this out for him. "The medical examiner found peanuts in his stomach." Then she emphasized, "But we didn't serve any appetizers made with peanuts."

"Not as part of the official menu, perhaps," Jackson agreed. "But you, Miss McNabb, were the last one into the party. Let's see. I believe you burned some appetizers...your reason for staying behind in the kitchen. That would have given you ample time to make up a deadly canapé or two."

"What?" Pippa was so frustrated she wanted to scream. Though she was obviously spinning her wheels with the hardheaded policeman, she said, "There's something you've forgotten about, Lieutenant."

"And that is?"

"I still didn't have a motive!" She jammed the receiver into its cradle, then jumped up when she realized she'd wedged a hip next to Sky's. Ignoring the unwelcome surge of heat shooting through her, she said, "That man makes me so nuts I could scream."

"So why don't you?"

"In a place of business?"

"Your door's closed," he said, his voice suddenly suggestive.

Her pulse thrummed. "Someone might think I'm being attacked." Her brother, for one. "Then you'll be in trouble again."

"I'm used to trouble."

But instead of shrieking, Pippa laughed humorlessly. "Jackson didn't believe me. Why not? Do I seem like a vicious person to you?"

Sky's gaze brushed the angles of her face, making unwanted, unwelcome warmth rise in Pippa all the way to her cheeks. But if he noticed the flags of color declaring her attraction to him, he ignored them for the moment. He said only, "Cops like keeping their cards close to their vest. Jackson was on a fishing expedition. Seeing if he could get you to say something you didn't mean to."

"That makes me feel a whole lot better," she muttered in disgust.

"Does it?"

Their gazes meshed, making Pippa want to melt, making her wish he'd offer her a shoulder rather than a challenge. Not that she would accept. She didn't want to give Sky Thornton any ideas. He already had too many of his own. Staring into those deep blue eyes, she could see one fomenting. She stiffened, but found she couldn't move.

Escape was impossible— It was too late. The eyes were drawing closer as was the rest of him, and she couldn't budge to save herself....

When Sky kept moving, brushing her with his arm as he reached for the medical examiner's report that she'd set on the desk on her other side, Pippa was mortified by her own imagination.

Only half-convinced that she was glad to escape another of his embraces, she pushed past Sky and returned to the safe side of the desk. Gratefully, since her legs were shaky, she plopped into her chair with a big sigh.

"Peanuts are a pretty recognizable item," Sky was saying, perusing the list again. "One would think Lamont would be aware of them because of his allergy."

"Unless there was something else mixed with the peanuts disguising them," Pippa suggested. "Celery and apples both crunch pretty well."

"They're both on the list."

She nodded. "We served both."

"And water chestnuts?" he queried.

She nodded. "In the rumaki."

"So someone could have substituted a few of the ingredients. Maybe made an appetizer that looked like something Birch had already eaten...except this one had a secret and lethal ingredient."

"Peanuts. But who?" Pippa thought hard, and an image she'd blocked out suddenly came to her. Her mouth dropped open. Could it be...? "Connie Ortega, the catering manager."

Sky's gaze narrowed. "The woman in charge yesterday, when you were locked in the storeroom...you think she did it?"

"I don't know. But Connie did slip something out of the refrigerator before taking a cart to the party. I didn't remember until just now."

"You didn't see what it was?"

Pippa shook her head. "Or I saw it but didn't think anything. I mean, it could have been an appetizer that looked identical to something already on her tray." And the afternoon before, Connie Ortega had had the opportunity to lock Pippa up while searching her jacket pocket for the film....

"Motive?"

There it was—the snag. Pippa sighed and sank back into the chair. "Your guess is as good as mine."

"Did she and Birch dislike each other?"

"How many times do I have to remind you that I didn't know Lamont very well." Another image niggled at her. "Wait a minute. Those files Frank Hatcher got out of Lamont's office yesterday..."

"What kind of files?"

"They seemed to be personnel files, with the employee name printed at the top. I saw several of the names. Connie's was one of them."

"So who's this Frank Hatcher?"

"The manager in data processing. He said he was picking up some data reports that Lamont wanted to see before they were finalized."

"Maybe we should go see Frank Hatcher."

"Not we. Me." Ignoring Sky's immediate scowl, Pippa insisted, "As his boss I can do it without raising all kinds of questions." Remembering the incident, she said, "Come to think of it, Frank was acting pretty suspiciously. Nervous. He did one of his habitual time checks and scooted out of there like someone was nipping at his heels."

"A little man, thinning hair?"

"Yes. You've met?"

"I saw him at the wake. He stood over the coffin like a little vulture, as if he was making sure Birch was dead. Then he took one look at his watch and scurried off."

She nodded. "Typical Frank Hatcher behavior when he's uncomfortable or worried about something."

"What could the manager of data processing have to worry about?"

"What, indeed?"

With the promise that she would fill him in later, Pippa encouraged Sky to leave so she could get down to business—detective business. If Lieutenant Isaac Jackson didn't want to do his job—if he thought for a moment he could pin a murder rap on her!—then she would gladly proceed with the investigation herself.

Unfortunately, Frank Hatcher had left for an early lunch, so her new line of work was delayed for the moment. Frustrated, she entered his office, anyway, and quickly found the stack of folders he'd taken from Lamont's office the day before.

Connie Ortega's was empty.

GWEN WALSH GLANCED UP from her half-empty plate. "I'm so glad I had the chance to treat you to lunch after all your help on the fund-raiser."

Pippa chewed her mouthful of food and swallowed before saying, "I have to admit, continuing to work after seeing someone buried is rather difficult." Then she appeared startled. "Oh, you weren't at the funeral. Or the wake."

Though the other woman didn't sound judgmental, Gwen chose to explain. "I'm not good with dead bodies. I was pretty young when my mother died in an institution, and I ended up handling the whole thing." That was part of the awful truth. "That kind of experience colors your viewpoint, you know?"

"I guess it would. Thankfully, I still have both my parents. What about your father?"

Gwen stiffened. "He walked before I was even born."
She hoped Pippa would stop there.

"I'm sorry."

The last thing she wanted was pity. "Can't miss what
you never had."

"Not even now? Around the holidays?"

Gwen was tempted to tell Pippa what she thought of
the holidays, but discretion got the better of her. "I'll
have plenty of people around. I'll be working the outdoor soup kitchen we're setting up both Christmas Eve
and part of Christmas Day."

"Doing something worthwhile." Pippa smiled. "I
guess you couldn't have a better holiday."

Oh, she could, but Gwen wasn't about to shock the
little innocent. Instead she changed the subject. "So
you like the food here?"

"Surprisingly so."

"Not everyone can get into vegetarian."

"That's because a lot of people think vegetarian food
is tasteless. You know, overcooked vegetables and bland
grains. This stuff is both crunchy and spicy. I can't even
identify everything in here. Water chestnuts and celery
and—"

"Who cares what's in it as long as it's delicious."
Gwen swallowed her final mouthful of the gourmet
platter and finally got to the real reason for the last-
minute lunch invitation. "Pippa, you haven't come
across any more coalition files, have you?"

"No. As far as I know, you have them all. If anyone
else at Westbrook's was working with Lamont on coalition business, he never said."

She was afraid of that. *Someone* had the information that could incriminate her, however. "What about
his widow?"

"Acacia? She did seem to take a particular interest in the fund-raiser."

Interest? Lamont's bitch of a wife had tried to make it seem as if she were the hostess, as if she were running the fund-raiser herself when she hadn't done diddly other than provide a list of socially correct invitees! It had taken all Gwen's willpower to hang back and let the socialite do whatever she chose when what she really wanted to do was to scratch out the bitch's eyes. After all, she hadn't wanted to upset things.

"Maybe Acacia was helping Lamont with some of his work at home," Gwen suggested.

"That's possible," Pippa agreed.

"Then you'll check with her?"

"I'm sure she'll be happy to turn over anything she has to you—"

Knowing that was the last thing that would make Acacia Birch happy, Gwen cut Pippa off. "I'd rather *you* asked, if you don't mind." And because the redhead appeared genuinely puzzled, she admitted, "That woman hates me. She wouldn't give me the time of day."

Pippa's eyebrows winged upward. "Sure. If things would be awkward for you, I'd be glad to." After hesitating a moment, she said, "I, uh, guess maybe I should offer *you* my condolences?"

At the unanticipated implication, Gwen's jaw dropped and she sat back and glared at Pippa. "You're joking! You can't believe...why, I wouldn't have taken up with Lamont Birch if he were the last man on earth!"

"I didn't mean—"

"Yes, you did!"

Gwen knew she needed to control her flaring temper before she put off her one sure ally. But she'd been so on edge for weeks that it was getting more and more difficult to remain calm in the face of adversity. If the police got hold of the file before she did, they would have reason to suspect her. If they thought she had been Lamont's mistress, as well...

Unable to help herself, she asked, "What are you trying to do, Pippa? Implicate me in Lamont's murder?"

Pippa's mouth dropped open. "Of course not. Whatever made you jump to that conclusion?"

"Oh, I can see the tabloids now. 'Jealous mistress kills lover because he wouldn't leave wife.'" She sucked in some air. "Lamont *was* having an affair, and his dear, narcissistic Acacia found out. She couldn't tolerate the idea that he desired another woman more than he did her."

She could practically hear Pippa's wheels spinning as she asked, "Lamont told you this?"

"Of course not."

Gwen forced herself to relax. Maybe she could still turn this conversation to her advantage. Merely by telling the truth, she could remove suspicion from herself and place it onto the affluent, coldhearted widow.

"Acacia and Lamont had a public argument about the affair," Gwen said with a properly sober expression. "It was at a meeting of the coalition's board of directors. There were tons of witnesses." She hesitated just a short moment so her next statement would have its full effect. "The argument climaxed with Acacia threatening to see Lamont dead before she so much as thought about granting him a divorce!"

"THE DIVORCE IS THE KEY!" Nola Yarbrough stated, her voice rising with her agitation. A frown creased her face with tiny lines that nearly made her look her true age despite several nips and tucks. "Have you asked her about it?"

Sky kept his temper in check. "Not yet."

"You don't sound as if you mean to."

"I'm doing this my way, remember."

Nola began pacing again, talking more to herself than to him. "You're taking too long. She'll suspect something. If you hadn't done things *your* way ten years ago—"

"Don't you dare blame me! I was the casualty in that one, remember?"

She stopped dead in her tracks and patted a phantom silver strand back into her coiffure. "Yes, of course I remember. Though you really shouldn't have taken it to heart the way you did."

Fury took his voice—along with his breath—away for a moment. What in the hell did she know about love? For her, husbands were as disposable a commodity as her furniture. He looked around. This husband was French Provincial. "Nola, if you're as smart as I know you are, you'll stop bugging me now," Sky warned her. "You know I didn't want to do this in the first place."

"I didn't twist your arm. I thought you wanted to know the truth."

"The desire for truth is the only thing that's making me continue with this deception."

Nola's blue eyes widened. "You're falling for her, aren't you?"

"I'm not falling for anyone," he said, perhaps a tad too quickly.

"Liar." Her carefully dyed silver brows arched. "I can hear it in your voice . . . see it in your eyes."

He denied it to her, just as he kept trying to deny it to himself. "What you think you hear and see are nothing more than frustrated hormones protesting all that time I spent alone in the wilderness."

"I hope so. For your sake." Hesitating only a second, she tried for the last word as she always did. "If you let her, she'll fool you like she did Dutch. And then where will you be?"

Where, indeed, but in a hell of his own making.

"WHERE ARE THEY?" Pippa asked, waving Connie Ortega's empty folder in front of Frank Hatcher's face.

The data processing manager popped out of his chair and squinted at his watch. "You'll have to excuse me, Ms. McNabb. I have a meeting—"

"Sit down!" Her vehemence surprising even her, Pippa caught her breath as Hatcher followed orders. "Now. Where are Connie Ortega's records?" She scanned the piles of materials stacked around the office—mostly other bulging file folders and computer printouts. "They weren't in here." She'd decided to pursue the issue despite her lunchtime conversation with Gwen. Acacia could wait; the missing contents couldn't.

Hatcher was staring at a spot directly below Pippa's chin. "I wouldn't know where they are."

"I think you do." She slapped the empty folder down on the desk in front of Hatcher, making the nervous data processing manager jump. "You took this file from Lamont Birch's office and removed the contents."

"Why would I do that?" he asked huffily.

"Nice try. You tell me. Neither of us is leaving this office until I know exactly what was in this folder."

For a moment, the little man looked as if he were ready to revolt. Then his belligerent expression crumpled. "All right. I did it. But it wasn't fair. No one deserves to be fired because of that cretin!"

"Fired?" Wondering if he was referring to Connie or to himself, Pippa was elated. She couldn't believe she'd made him crack so easily. "For what?"

Jaw tightening, he turned to the bookcase behind him, muttering, "I should have burned it instead of putting it in a fireproof safe." Swinging open a section of shelving holding books, he attacked the small metal vault behind it. He zoomed through the combination, removed some sheaves of paper from the interior, then slammed the door before she could get a look inside. "Here."

Pippa scanned the top page—Connie Ortega's employment application. "Why did you remove this?"

"Keep going."

She flipped through several letters of recommendation and glowing yearly evaluations to a computerized police report. Pippa started. Nearly two decades before, a teenage Constance Ortega had been arrested with her boyfriend in a stolen car after crossing a state line. Despite the boyfriend's backing Connie's testimony that she'd known nothing about the theft, she'd spent several months in jail as an accessory to the crime.

Like many cash businesses, Westbrook's no longer hired anyone who'd been found guilty of theft. Pippa returned to the section of the employment application that specifically asked the potential worker whether or not he or she had ever been incarcerated. Connie had denied it.

"Lamont Birch forced me to do it," Hatcher was complaining.

"Do what exactly?"

"Get that information on Connie like he did on all the managers. He made me tap into all kinds of data banks."

A chill shot through her. Lamont playing *Big Brother?* "Why?"

"He was a control freak. He wanted something on everyone."

"What did he have on you?"

"He knew about my dealings with Dutch."

Hatcher had secretly bought up shares of stock for her late husband, part of Dutch's plan to gain controlling interest in the store.

"That's ancient history," she said, finally sinking into a chair opposite him. "My brother decided to give you another chance."

"But Birch said he could get Mr. McNabb to believe otherwise." Hatcher ran a shaky hand through his thinning hair, leaving a tuft standing straight up. "About my loyalty to him and you, that is. He said if I didn't do what he wanted, he'd make you believe I was selling confidential information to our competitors."

Pippa felt dazed. Lamont Birch a blackmailer. Not exactly the nice man he'd seemed to be. No wonder no one had truly seemed to mourn him. She wondered how many people like Frank Hatcher he'd had under his thumb. "How many people did he make you run computer checks on?" she asked.

"Want to see yours?" Hatcher returned.

At which Pippa's jaw dropped for the second time in one day. An employee had had the nerve to investigate *her?* If he weren't already dead . . . well, she'd at least give him a piece of her mind before firing him. *Fire . . .*

Lamont had gotten Hatcher to do what he wanted with that threat. Maybe he'd used it on lots of others. To what end? Just to be a secret power-monger? More likely there'd been another, bigger reason . . . a master plan in the works . . . one that someone decided to stop before it went any further.

Suddenly, the reason for Lamont's murder seemed to be even more elusive. There could be several people whose secrets he'd finagled through Frank Hatcher. Like Connie Ortega's. Remembering her suspicions about the catering manager, Pippa wondered exactly how far Lamont had pushed Connie with the information he'd obtained about her prison record.

Chapter Eight

"Probably not as far as you're imagining," Sky said that evening when she voiced that same question about Connie to him. They were on the way to Winnetka to see Acacia Birch.

"How can you be so certain?"

"She's a competent employee, right?"

"Definitely. She can be a bit strident, but she does her job superbly."

"And you and Rand are pretty open-minded, right?"

"I'd like to think so."

"She probably does, too. Chances are you wouldn't fire her for lying on her application about something that happened twenty years ago. And, more importantly, the stakes aren't high enough. The possibility of losing a job, even in this economy, isn't a strong enough reason to kill someone."

"True." She'd pretty much thought the same herself. "With her qualifications and experience, Connie wouldn't have much difficulty finding another job, anyway. Most employers would probably overlook the incident."

The darkness surrounding them as their route snaked and dipped through wooded areas where the mansions were all but obliterated from sight made Pippa shift uncomfortably. She couldn't help remembering last night's encounter. Her head throbbed anew from thinking about it.

Thankfully, they were almost to their destination— Chicago, Evanston and Wilmette were already behind them, and Kennilworth mansions now lined both sides of the road. Winnetka was just ahead. Access to the lakefront on their right was blocked by estates, many with coach houses and swimming pools or tennis courts. Though she'd never seen it herself, she knew Acacia Birch's family home would be equally grandiose.

"I'm glad I don't have to do this alone," Pippa admitted, struggling with her insecurities once more. Dutch had so often told her she wasn't competent to do anything right that she had to fight to believe otherwise. "I feel much better having you with me." And was annoyed with herself for saying it.

"Whoa! Careful," he said, reaching over and closing a hand over hers. "You might shock me into losing control."

At his touch, her pulse jumped and beat furiously in her throat. "Of the car? Or yourself?"

Though Pippa extricated her hand from his, the imprint of Sky's fingers surrounding hers lingered. Stressed by her growing attraction to him nearly as much as she was by the mystery, she managed to follow her unfriendly action with a weak grin that quickly faded when he didn't respond.

"I feel a little weird imposing on a widow on the night of her husband's burial," she said.

"I wouldn't worry about it since that widow wasn't too broken up either at the wake or the funeral."

"True. And this isn't a social call."

And her freedom was at stake—hers and Sky's. So she was willing to make allowances. Besides which, she'd already blown two possible leads for the day. She'd shown up at catering, after all, in the hopes of getting Connie alone. Too late. A crisis had intervened. When the prime rib for the mayor's public relations luncheon the next afternoon hadn't arrived on schedule—the truck had broken down en route to Westbrook's—Connie had left the store to pick up the meat herself.

A frustrated Pippa felt as if she'd had to do *something* positive, especially after arriving at the photo shop a few minutes too late. Closed for the day. Disappointment number two.

Seeing as Acacia was on her list, and as she had the perfect excuse—those coalition files Gwen was looking for—Pippa had decided to head for the North Shore and see what she could wring out of the widow about her late husband's unethical practices. Slouched in the front seat of his Ford Ranger, which he'd parked in her driveway, Sky had been waiting for her when she'd returned home to change. She'd been inordinately glad to see him.

"Here it is," he said, turning his vehicle through an opening in the fence.

On the lake side of the road, the huge lot was densely wooded and drifted over with snow. They left the four-wheeler at the back of the driveway next to a racy red Jaguar Pippa had never seen before. They crossed patches of ice hidden under the dusting of snow. When Pippa's foot slid out from under her, Sky grabbed her upper arm and anchored her. She was pressed against him. Chest to chest. Breath to breath.

Grateful that he'd prevented her fall, Pippa muttered, "Thanks," pushed at his chest and tried to remove her arm. She might as well have tried to shake off a bulldog.

She ignored the discomfort his touch caused and concentrated on the main building, a monstrous brick colonial home. Its huge windows were well lit, and raucous Latin music cut through the quiet of the night.

"Hmm, sounds more like a celebration than a dirge," Sky mused as they neared the pillared front entry.

"Some cultures do believe in giving the loved one an animated send-off," Pippa said, thinking of a few Irish wakes she'd been to over the years.

Sky merely grunted in response and pressed the buzzer several times in succession.

While they waited for a servant to answer the door, Pippa glanced down at the lake's frozen shoreline. Rather than smooth, the surface had been frozen into tortured shapes, as if the water had been trying to escape some pursuer when caught by the deep freeze. Thinking she was being too fanciful again—and reminded of her attack the night before—Pippa hugged her jacket tighter around her.

The door was flung open, but rather than a servant, Acacia herself stood there, teetering in the doorway, resplendent in a crimson beaded gown that clung to her svelte figure. The garment was cut so low in front that it almost revealed her navel and was slit so high that it did expose her thigh. Her dark, silver-streaked hair was loose around her bared shoulders.

Acacia quickly covered the distaste with which she received these unexpected visitors by hiding behind a bulbous crystal glass filled with amber liquid.

"Who is it, darling?" a man's deep voice called out over the music.

Making a strangled sound, she gulped some of the liquor and said, "Dear Lamont's employer," sending alcoholic fumes straight into Pippa's face.

The music died.

And Pippa closed her gaping mouth, firming it into a reasonable facsimile of a smile. "Acacia, you remember Sky Thornton, don't you?"

"We've met." Her dark gaze flashed in his direction. "What can I do for you?"

"Not for us exactly," Sky said.

Pippa explained, "For the Coalition to Feed the Homeless."

She spotted a man who was at least a dozen years Acacia's junior sneaking up the central staircase on the other side of the two-story reception hall. He was tall, dark, handsome and very dramatically Latin.

Undoubtedly realizing the situation at hand didn't have her full attention, Sky squeezed Pippa's arm and said, "We wouldn't have bothered you tonight if it hadn't been important."

"Right," Pippa agreed. Glancing over Acacia's bared shoulder, she could see into the living room, where an intimate dinner for two had been laid out before the roaring fireplace. It took all her willpower not to gawk. "But perhaps this is a bad time," she mumbled.

"Eduardo is my dance instructor. He was merely trying to cheer me up," Acacia said, making a face that Pippa figured was supposed to indicate that deep down the widow was grieving her heart out.

Feeling much better about her timing, Pippa asked, "May we come in?"

"Yes, of course. Where are my manners?"

Pippa didn't miss the malevolent glare the other woman aimed her way as Pippa led the way inside, tracking traces of snow across the perfectly polished marble floor.

"So what is this about the coalition?"

Was Acacia's voice really tight, Pippa wondered, or was she herself coloring what in fact had been a simple and expected question? "Gwen is looking for some missing records," she explained. "She thinks Lamont might have brought them home to work on coalition business."

"That is possible. I have my own charities," Acacia added quickly. "I didn't interfere with Lamont's."

"If he did bring coalition business home, where would he have kept it?" Sky asked.

"In his study, of course." Resigned, Acacia said, "I suppose you want to take a look."

"That would be helpful."

Pippa forced another smile and wondered how helpful Acacia would be under the circumstances. No doubt the woman would want them out of her house as quickly as possible so she could get back to her...dance instructor.

Pippa began chattering. "Gwen Walsh would like to find another legal counsel for the coalition as quickly as possible, and she says she needs the records in order to give the candidates an informed overview."

"Yes, well..." Acacia took another sip of her drink. "The sooner we look—"

"The sooner we'll be out of here," Sky finished for her.

"This way."

Hips swinging lushly, Acacia Birch led them to a closed door opposite the living room. Inside, she flicked a switch that turned on several strategically placed brass and glass desk lamps.

Lamont's study was lined with shelves that groaned with heavy, beautifully bound books that looked to be mostly about law. A fireplace and black leather seating arrangement decorated one end of the room, a mahogany desk, credenza and high-backed leather chair the other.

Acacia waved her glass to the work side of the room. "Help yourselves. The credenza is really a horizontal filing system. I'll be back after I attend to Eduardo."

The door had barely closed behind her before Sky muttered, "Define 'attend to.'"

"I can't believe she'd be so obvious. What will people think?"

"Does she care?"

Pippa frowned. "There *is* a murder investigation going on."

"Speaking of investigating . . ."

"Let's get to it."

Removing their winter gear and throwing them on a chair, Pippa started with the desk while Sky took the first file drawer. While Acacia obviously had no loyalties to her late husband, neither did she seem to have reason to turn them away. She'd not only opened Lamont's study to them, but had left them alone.

Apparently Acacia Birch had nothing to hide—or fear.

A COMBINATION OF ANGER and deep-seated fear drove Acacia up the stairs and into the bedroom, where she threw open the door. "Are you insane?"

Eduardo lay sprawled across the bed. Naked. Ready. He raised his glass to her. "Insane for you, my lovely one. Come, take your clothes off. Let me kiss that frown from your magnificent face."

Normally her new lover could seduce her into anything. Tonight he merely made her want to scream. "It's bad enough they saw you…us. If they were to hear…"

He rose up on an elbow. "You did not get rid of them?"

"I couldn't exactly throw them out."

Though she'd wanted to when she'd seen the looks on their faces. How dare Pippa and this Thornton man judge her when they didn't know what she'd gone through living with Lamont for more than a decade— more than a decade too long. Marrying him had been her worst nightmare come true.

Well, maybe not her worst. If she weren't careful, that could still happen, Acacia realized. No. She wouldn't let it happen. She'd have to be very, very clever to keep in control of the situation. Because now that Lamont was out of her hair for good, she was planning on enjoying her widowhood and was looking forward to making up for the years wasted by her marriage—a bad joke that fate had played on her.

And neither Pippa McNabb nor Sky Thornton had better get in her face to ruin her plans!

SITTING COMFORTABLY in the high-backed leather chair, Sky stared down at a familiar-looking face. "Keegan. Well, well, what do you know—Lamont Birch was keeping quite a file on Mayor Darby Keegan."

"What?"

Pippa set down the coalition folders they'd just found and crowded him for a look as he began thumbing through the newspaper clippings. Her scent teased him. And a silky curl brushed his cheek enticingly. Everything about Pippa was making him restless. He wanted nothing more than to set aside whatever Birch had gotten on the mayor and pull her into his lap so he could taste her mouth again.

Instead he clenched his jaw and paged through faster. "There must be more than a hundred stories on Keegan here," he said, noting clippings on his involvement with the city council and neighborhood meetings, on his appearances at ground breakings and museum exhibit openings, on his opinions about gang violence and the need for casinos to fund the city treasury. "What's the fascination?"

"Hmm. The night he died, Lamont said something about running for mayor himself," Pippa mused, the soft flesh of her hip and thigh pressing against his arm, effectively distracting him. "And there was something else . . . something about Keegan ending up with mud in his face, though he admitted that wasn't the night to do it. Not that any of the argument made sense, since Lamont didn't live in Chicago."

Sky was having trouble making sense of anything at the moment. Especially of his feelings. Pressing back against Pippa, all his faculties filling with her essence, he kept enough presence of mind to ask, "Then why collect this stuff as if it's proof?" as he locked gazes with her.

For a moment, the only thing between them was awareness. . . .

Then, a flat-sounding "Proof of what?" from the other side of the room broke the momentary spell.

Pippa's eyes widened and she jumped away from him. Sky craned around to see Acacia Birch glide into the room. She'd changed into a modest black jumpsuit and had swept her hair back into a simple French knot.

She would look quite elegant if her features weren't so taut. Did she fear he'd found something he shouldn't have? "Proof that your late husband had some weird fascination with Darby Keegan."

Acacia's expression immediately relaxed and her dark eyebrows shot upward. "Lamont made an avocation of hating Keegan. And of wanting his job."

"But how did he think he could run for mayor of Chicago when he lived in Winnetka?" Pippa asked.

"Because of a simple technicality." Acacia wandered toward the desk, her gaze immediately lighting on the clippings. "Lamont never sold his city apartment after we married. For all intents and purposes, he lived here. But he continued claiming his Chicago apartment as his primary residence to the IRS...though he primarily used the place for his mail delivery...and other interests."

Sky wondered if Pippa had known about Birch's city residence. And from what she'd just told him about the argument on the night of the murder, he also suspected that the lawyer had gotten something incriminating on the mayor—attaining information that gave him a hold over people had obviously been Birch's passion—and if so, perhaps that incriminating data was in this particular file. It would take hours to sort through the details properly, he realized.

"You wouldn't have any objection to our borrowing this, would you?" Sky inquired of the widow.

Acacia seemed about to agree. Then she frowned and protested, "Wait a minute. You said you were here to look for coalition materials."

"I found several folders." Pippa indicated the short stack on the desk.

"I ran across this one by accident," Sky explained, "and I'm thinking it might have some information that could be very helpful."

"Helpful?"

"In clearing *our* names." He watched the subtle transformation of Acacia's expression from considering . . . to downright cunning.

"Lamont *was* dedicated to getting Darby Keegan out of office, and I'm afraid he didn't care how," Acacia said slowly. "Do you think the mayor might have avenged himself by killing my dear, departed husband?"

At the moment, Sky was wondering if she might not have done the dirty deed herself and was looking to place the blame elsewhere. But, not wanting to cross Acacia and thereby cut off her help in the event they needed her cooperation, he simply said, "Anything is possible."

"Well, then, by all means, take as long and hard a look as you must."

Long and hard enough so that he could find a way to divert suspicion from *her?* Whatever Acacia's reasoning, Sky was thankful she was choosing to be cooperative. It wouldn't hurt to cover all their bases.

"Well, we got what we came for," he said. *And more.* "We probably should let you get some . . . rest."

"How thoughtful. Yes, it would be best if you left now."

Pippa frowned. "But first I'd like to—"

Sky cut off her protest with a hard squeeze and amended quickly, "But first we *both* want to thank you," before she had the chance to say something that might change the widow's mind.

"Thank *you*," Acacia echoed with a brilliant smile, which made her look like she really meant it.

Meanwhile, Pippa struggled to free herself. She elbowed her way out of Sky's firm grip and gave him a dirty look. Then she smiled sweetly at Acacia. "Gwen will be relieved to get these, I'm sure," she said, indicating the stack of coalition folders before slipping into her coat. She wouldn't even look his way.

Sky threw on his jacket and was bundling up when Acacia said, "If you find anything *interesting* about Mayor Keegan, I hope I'll be the first to know."

"Who else would we tell?" Sky said noncommittally. *Other than the police, of course.*

Pippa didn't counter him. She didn't say anything. It wasn't until they were in the Ranger and headed for home that she finally spoke. "What was the big idea of shutting me up?" she demanded. "I wanted to question Acacia, to find out how much she knew about Lamont's unethical practices."

"I figured as much, but I thought your timing was a little off."

"My timing was perfect!"

Patiently he explained, "I wanted to get out of there *with* that folder on Keegan."

"Who's to say you wouldn't have?" she countered.

"We can start looking through those clippings as soon as we get to your place."

Plainly irritated that he was trying to change the subject, she stubbornly insisted, "I can't."

"Why not? You have a hot date?"

"I need to take a shower and wash my hair... if you don't mind."

"So take a shower." That would work perfectly. Give him enough time to do some exploring. He'd been waiting for this opportunity. "Take a nice, long shower, wash your hair twice if you want, and then we'll get down to work again. We'll stop any time you're ready for bed," he said, the statement inadvertently conjuring up images that stirred him against his better judgment. "Any more objections?"

"Only to your acting as if I didn't know how to conduct myself without putting off Acacia," she said, bringing the argument full circle. "Besides which, you didn't have to be so rude!"

"I did the first thing that came to mind."

"Force. Running right over me . . . just like my late husband," she muttered.

Sky started and grasped the steering wheel even harder. He hated the comparison. He glanced at Pippa, but she was pointedly avoiding him by staring out her window.

Dutch running over her? It was supposed to be the other way around, at least according to Nola. Then again, he'd already realized Pippa McNabb wasn't exactly the grasping, resourceful and underhanded woman as described. Did Nola really believe all the negative things she'd said about Pippa? Or did Nola's loyalty to her dead son prompt her to continue to take his side against the young wife who had intended to divorce him? Obviously Nola hadn't been able to see the truth, even given a year to mourn. She'd chosen not to reconcile her feelings for Dutch with the real man he'd been.

The truth smacked Sky unpleasantly. Pippa really was closer to being the innocent he'd first imagined than the viper Nola had portrayed. That didn't give him any easy way out, though. In fact, it made things harder. He was falling for Pippa, but he had to see the plan through. Had to find out whether or not Nola had been telling the truth about Dutch any more than she had about Pippa.

Then what?

What did it matter if Pippa found out now or later? For he was certain she *would* find out, no matter what. And either way, she would hate him. It was only a matter of time. Suddenly he realized that seeing her hurt and feeling her hatred would surely destroy him.

Truth was, he was more than falling... he was down for the count. What a hell of a quandary. He could delay the inevitable, but he couldn't change who he was.

And it wouldn't be the first time he'd lost a woman he loved because of Dutch Vanleer.

As PIPPA STRIPPED OFF her clothes, negative memories of Dutch preyed on her mind, undoubtedly because she was so attracted to Sky... and was equally disappointed in him. That maneuver with Acacia had reminded her of her late husband's contempt. Where did he get off acting as if she didn't have the brains to handle a delicate situation?

She slipped into a plush crimson terry robe and headed for the bathroom, angry with herself for allowing Sky to stay. He was downstairs in the living room, waiting for her to take that shower and wash her hair.

He'd won—and she hated that she'd let him.

Pippa turned on the shower, then shivered when the spray of icy water assaulted her. It would take a few minutes for the hot water to make its way from the tank in the basement to the second floor. That would give her enough time to evict Sky Thornton from the premises.

With that in mind, she secured the robe's sash and, shower left running, made her way down the stairs in bare feet. But oddly, Sky wasn't waiting for her. She wandered into the empty living room. The folder with the clippings about Mayor Keegan still lay on the coffee table. Surely Sky wouldn't have left his precious information behind had he changed his mind about staying.

Her heart thudded, yet fear kept her from calling out. What if her attacker had returned and Sky was after him? Or worse—the other way around. What if Sky had already been silenced? The thought made her act instantly, if cautiously, as she began checking the premises.

From where she stood, she could see straight into the dining room. Empty. Shifting to her right a few feet, she had a clear shot at the kitchen. No one there, either, and the back door seemed properly secured. Carefully moving in the opposite direction—toward the front of the house—she next inspected the parlor. Unoccupied.

But a slash of light cut through the darkened hall on that side of the main staircase. Drawn to it like a moth to a flame, she noted the door to the study was slightly ajar. Bright light outlined the wooden panel, though no untoward sounds came from within. Could Sky be in there? More importantly, was he alone? And conscious? As much as he chose to press her buttons, as angry as she'd been with him, Pippa couldn't tolerate the idea of seeing Sky hurt.

Stepping carefully so as to give no warning, she crossed to the study, peeked through the crack, and when she still didn't see him, eased the door open. Her heart was in her throat, and her fear drove a rushing sound through her head that drowned out the muffled noise of the shower upstairs.

A moment's relief—he was alone, his back to her.

She calmed down immediately, swallowed hard, took a deep breath and chastised herself for being so foolish—for wanting to run her fingers through the thick black hair that nestled around his neck and to tell him how glad she was that he was all right.

Then she realized he was sitting at Dutch's desk. Going through Dutch's drawers. Searching Dutch's things. She'd avoided her late husband's study like the plague, so every item inside had been his. And now Sky was looking for something ... but what?

"What are you doing?" she demanded to know, boldly stepping into the room.

He whipped around. "I thought you were taking a shower." He made a face. "The shower's still going."

And undoubtedly shooting all her hot water directly down the drain, she thought, barely cognizant of the muted sound. While only minutes ago, fear had made her head buzz, now anger did the same. "We're not talking about me." The sheaf of papers in his hand mesmerized her. "What are you doing in here?" She indicated the documents he had no right to touch. "What do you expect to find?"

He immediately dropped the papers onto the desk and rose. "This is your late husband's study, isn't it?"

"Exactly."

"You've made some unflattering comments about Dutch ... and then you've compared me to him," he said, moving closer. "I wanted to learn everything I could about the man who didn't deserve to be your husband."

Staring at his solemn expression, she half believed him, though she didn't know why she should. Perhaps because she needed to. "So why didn't you just ask?" And why was her heart pounding out of control again?

"Dredging up old hurts can be painful."

"You were trying to spare me?" She forced a laugh. "Come now."

"I have no desire to see you in pain."

Again she believed him. And had trouble swallowing. "Why?" she croaked, though she'd felt the same for him.

He stopped so close that his body heat caressed her. Wanting to respond—thinking she had to be crazy—she stared down at her bare toes.

"Because I couldn't tolerate knowing I was the cause."

Sensing he really meant that, she shifted uncomfortably and met his hot blue gaze. "Why?" she asked again.

"Can't you guess?"

He slid a hand behind her neck and drew her forward, quickly closing the gap between their faces. Then he covered her mouth with his.

Pippa responded instantly and fully to the hot, wet kiss. She hooked her arms around his neck and drew her fingers through his longish hair. She got almost as much pleasure from its texture as she did from Sky's mouth.

He was an all-or-nothing kind of man. He took rather than asked. Plundered rather than explored. He boldly slid his tongue along the sensitive crevices of her mouth . . . and even more boldly ran his hand along her vulnerable inner thigh. Her robe had loosened, and he took advantage, inserting himself, his rough clothing rubbing against her tender flesh. Thrills bolted straight to her center, and when he traced a callused hand up her belly, she moaned with pleasure.

But when he found her breast, her heart raced too fast, scaring her. Thinking surely the pleasure would make her burst from the inside out, she broke the kiss, came up for air . . . feeling like a wanton in his arms.

And then she realized where she was—Dutch's study. She had avoided this seeming embodiment of her late husband, had entered only when and for as long as necessary. Now here she was, flushed and aroused, robe split, another man's hand stroking her pebbled flesh. She wasn't even thinking straight.

Head clearing, Pippa jerked away and wrapped the terry tightly around herself.

Sky protested. "Don't—"

"I don't even know you," she gasped, wondering what had come over her. "You're a stranger."

"You've known me for days. And I've told you about myself."

"That you're a naturalist and an expert in survival skills." He was also an expert with women, as he'd just demonstrated. "Surface stuff. It doesn't tell me who you are. What you feel. Where you live." She started and complained, "Where *do* you live? I have no idea of where you're staying here in town."

His mouth curled into that familiar smile. "Maybe it's time I showed you. Tomorrow night?"

She knew she ought to turn him down. Ought to, but didn't want to. She wanted to know everything about him. Wanted more than a taste of his loving.

"All right." Her heart thumped to an odd inner tune. "Where do I go? What time?"

"Whoa. You're racing ahead of yourself. Tomorrow's a long day." His voice was seductive. "And I plan on seeing you for as much of it as possible."

Her pulse skipped. "You mean you're going to hang around Westbrook's again?" Meaning she wouldn't get any work done. Again.

"How else am I going to conduct a private investigation?"

"You make it sound like you're on your own, Sky. I thought we were in this thing together."

"Exactly."

In an effort to free herself from a trap of her own making, she contended, "That doesn't mean we have to spend every minute together."

"What do you suggest?"

"You follow up on your leads," she said, thinking of the folder on Keegan, "and I'll follow up on mine." Starting first thing in the morning by recovering the prints made from the roll of film she'd found. Hopefully, they would have nothing to do with Sky. She'd almost forgotten she'd ever suspected him, and now she thought doing so just might keep her sane a while longer.

"Your leads?" His eyebrows arched. "Holding something back, are we?"

Refusing to admit as much, Pippa backed away slightly, then fibbed, "I was thinking about having a talk with Connie." Not a half-bad idea.

"I thought we agreed her motivation wasn't strong enough."

"*If* we know the whole story." Pippa still wondered about the catering manager's peculiar actions. "So I'll follow up with Connie and you'll take on the mayor."

"Deal. And we'll share everything over dinner tomorrow night at my place."

"Where—"

"I'll take you there. Agreed?"

Crushing her terry robe closer, Pippa nodded, telling herself she hadn't made a pact with the devil.

Chapter Nine

Having a devil of a time finding a legal parking spot on Broadway the next morning, Pippa was relieved when another car pulled out of its space a little more than a block from Broadway Photo Finishers. The green Civic that she'd seen more than once since leaving her garage rolled to a standstill behind her. *Damn!* The driver had better not be planning on trying to steal her spot, an all-too-common occurrence in a neighborhood where parking was at a premium, especially when several inches of snow covered the ground.

She carefully watched the other car in her rearview mirror as she edged up to align herself with one that was parked, then eased back into the space. To her relief, the Civic sped on by before she came to a halt next to the ice-covered curb.

Clambering out, Pippa noted the other driver was parking illegally in a loading zone several lengths ahead. Oh, well. His ticket. She slammed the car door and was starting off when she realized the other driver had left his car, as well, and was now rushing in her direction.

Her eyes popped at both his size and getup—a dwarf, or little person, to be politically correct, dressed like a Christmas elf. Belying the spirit of the holiday, his rough-hewn features were drawn into a scowl, his lips pulled into a thin line. He glanced her way and, giving her a hostile expression, veered off toward the sidewalk and a nearby shop. Telling herself to forget about it, Pippa headed for the photo shop, eager to see what had developed.

Ahead of her, a bell tinkled steadily. On the corner stood a guy from the Salvation Army. He was wearing a Santa Claus outfit. She faltered, gave Santa an intense look, then told herself to stop being ridiculous. If she expected to see Lamont behind the beard, she wouldn't. Lamont was dead and buried. And she couldn't get freaked out every time she saw a man in a fuzzy red suit—at least not at this time of the year. Digging in her pockets, she came up with some change and dumped it into the man's pot as she passed by.

"Merry Christmas, young lady!" Santa called after her in a hearty voice.

She had just looked back to return the greeting when she spotted the elf once more headed in her direction. Her smile faded.

A weird sensation gripping her, Pippa speeded up, glancing over her shoulder to check on the little man's progress. Could he possibly be following her? He was moving every bit as fast as she was, his small feet kicking up a storm of crunchy snow. He glared at her again and stopped to speak to Santa . . . and Pippa felt like a fool for the second time. Obviously, he was merely another costumed Salvation Army volunteer.

A moment later, she was snug and warm inside the store and claiming the developed photographs.

"That'll be eight dollars and seventy-three cents," the clerk told her.

Pippa dug into her wallet and pulled out a ten, nearly anxious enough to rip open the package right there. But she had already determined to wait until she returned to the privacy of her own car. Whatever the photos revealed would be for her eyes alone.

Suddenly the hair on the back of her neck rose, and some instinct compelled her to whip her head toward the storefront window just as someone whisked by and out of sight. She imagined the person to be wearing a familiar dark green. The elf again? Spying on her? Surely not.

"Here you go, ma'am."

"Thanks. Have a good holiday."

Pippa took her change and dumped it into her wallet, which she then stuffed into her shoulder bag along with the packet of photographs. Her instinct for self-preservation alive and well, she crossed the strap over her body and positioned the leather pouch where she could hang on to it with both hands. Then, feeling like a trained urban guerrilla, she stalked out of the store, rubbernecking for trouble.

But once on the street, she was calling herself a nincompoop as well as other unflattering names. The only other person on foot nearby was Santa. She grinned weakly as she passed him.

Safely locked into her car a couple of minutes later, she was able to relax completely. She had to stop seeing bogeymen where there were none.

Removing her shoulder bag, Pippa immediately opened the flap and pulled out the packet. Her pulse quickened and her chest tightened in anticipation. She prayed she'd find nothing inside that would implicate Sky. Hand shaking, she removed the first photograph...and stared at a shot of two small children posed before a holiday window display.

Kids? Christmas decorations? Her pulse raced faster than the eight reindeer involved in Lamont's death. What the heck kind of incriminating evidence was this? Frustrated, Pippa dumped the contents of the packet into her lap and quickly spread out the photographs. But none were any more revealing than the first. All were similar pictures of the downtown area with what appeared to be a mom, dad and their two kids posing in different combinations.

"Damn!" All that hype over a roll of film dropped by someone on a family outing rather than by the person who'd been arguing with Lamont—Pippa couldn't believe she'd gotten her hopes up for nothing.

Her letdown was so complete that she angrily shoved the photos back together and crammed them into their envelope, wishing she'd never found the darn roll of film in the first place. It wasn't until she threw the packet onto the passenger seat that the hair on her nape stood at attention once more. She swiveled around fast, but survey the area as she would, Pippa couldn't spot anyone near the car.

Still...her flesh crawled and she couldn't rid herself of the idea that someone really had been there. Could she really have imagined being watched twice? Maybe...but why take any chances?

No sooner did Pippa crank the engine than she started to pull out of her parking space. She was momentarily distracted by what looked to be a flash of dark green in the sideview mirror. She craned over her shoulder but saw nothing...especially not the oncoming vehicle.

The blare of a warning horn triggered her automatic reflexes. She stomped the brake pedal—hard—to the floor. Her own car bucked to a stop, brakes shrieking, as a van barreled by with mere inches to spare. The driver swung around to glare at her, his mouth moving, no doubt forming a curse. And how could she blame him?

She waited a moment for her heart to leave her throat and settle back in her chest where it belonged. Then after cautiously checking for oncoming traffic, Pippa finished pulling away from the curb, noting the green Civic was still in the loading zone. She glanced in her rearview mirror several times in the space of the next block to make certain it didn't follow.

Nearly a half hour later, she pulled into the alley with the loading dock that split Westbrook's first floor in two and claimed the last of the empty slots provided for top management. As she grabbed her bag, she saw the photographs had slipped from the packet. They were spread, facedown, across the driver's seat.

Shaking her head at her own foolishness, she left them where they lay, determined the day wouldn't be a total loss where her private investigation was concerned.

"LIEUTENANT JACKSON hasn't gotten any further with his official investigation," Rand grumbled to Pippa later that morning.

"Why should he try when he's satisfied with his suspects?" She was working in catering, setting up the private dining room for the mayor's press luncheon, waiting for her opportunity to speak to Connie alone. Her brother had stopped by to see how they were coming along, and she'd made the mistake of asking if he'd spoken to the detective.

"Don't worry. He's not going to railroad you into a trial if I have anything to say about it. If all else fails...I'm not a half-bad amateur sleuth, remember."

She did remember. He'd helped solve Dutch's murder—he and Shelby. "Maybe it runs in the family," she said, thinking she should tell him how she'd learned about Lamont's hobby of keeping unofficial records on people.

But when he said, "Don't go getting any ideas," she changed her mind.

"No, of course not," she said coolly, setting two silver servers filled with salad dressing opposite each other on a linen-covered table.

Naturally her big brother wouldn't want her to assert herself, to take a stand, to get herself in trouble, for heaven's sake. She'd been considering filling him in on her and Sky's investigation and asking for his opinion. She'd also been thinking of asking his advice about Sky. Rand had pegged Dutch right, only then she hadn't been willing to listen. And now, given his quick disapproval, she wasn't willing to ask him anything.

"Listen, Rand," Pippa said, picking up two more boats of salad dressing, "I've got to get back to work here before Connie gives me the evil eye."

He nodded and made a face. "Start thinking about promoting yourself, about kicking yourself upstairs where you belong, starting in the new year. I promise I'll make sure things go easy for you. How about it?"

"I'll think it over."

Pippa set the salad dressing in place on the next table. She would kick herself upstairs only when she could take over her share of the work as a full partner. *Easy* was a cop-out.

Rand gave her a quick hug. "Don't work too hard."

Pippa was relieved to see him go. She *wanted* to work hard. Crossing in front of the Christmas tree decorating the corner of the room, she also resolved to work harder on solving Lamont's murder. When Connie asked her for some help a few minutes later, Pippa jumped at her chance. She followed the manager back to the catering department.

"Here's the seating arrangement," Connie began, picking up a clipboard from the hall desk. "I need—"

"What did you think of Lamont Birch?" Pippa interrupted.

Caution shadowed the other woman's expression and she hesitated. Then, when she spoke, her voice was edgy. "I didn't know him well."

"I'll bet you knew him well enough to form an opinion."

"What makes you so certain?"

Hoping for the catering manager's gut reaction without having to spill the beans—she wanted to make certain Connie knew that Lamont had dug into her past—all Pippa said was, "Frank Hatcher."

"Oh, God." Gripping the clipboard to her breast, Connie sank into a chair, her reaction confirming the connection. "You know."

Pippa merely nodded. And waited. Connie's complexion had gone pasty and she appeared ready to hyperventilate.

"Do I at least get two weeks' notice?"

It was Pippa's turn to be startled. "What?"

"You're going to fire me, aren't you?"

"I wasn't planning on it."

"But my application…" Connie's eyes widened. "We are talking about the same thing, aren't we?"

"You're referring to omitting your police record?"

"Damn!" Connie slapped the clipboard down on the desk. "I was a dumb kid in love, for God's sake. And I had nothing to do with the theft. I didn't even know the car was stolen."

"Is that what you told Lamont?"

"Yes, but he didn't believe me, either. That's why I started looking for a new job. I wanted references before Birch could spread his poison and get me fired."

"What did he want you to do to keep quiet?"

Again the hesitation. "I don't understand."

"What was the price for his silence?"

Connie took a deep breath. "He said there might be times when I could make an effort to pick up information… listen to conversations during certain events … you know how it is. Catering employees are invisible to the customers when they become self-involved."

"So did you?"

"No. Birch never got the chance to force the issue."

"And you're thankful for that."

"Who wouldn't be? I would have done anything to avoid his using me."

"Anything?" Pippa asked, à la Lieutenant Isaac Jackson.

Connie's eyes widened again. "You don't think *I*…"

But instead of being freaked out, the catering manager laughed. Pippa was not amused. "Why not you?"

"You really think anyone in their right mind would kill someone over a job?" She seemed astounded. "Are you serious? Not everyone would hold my background against me. I could get another position like … well, it might not be that easy, but I could get one."

The very same conclusion Sky had come to. Pippa was more than half-convinced Connie was innocent of murder, but now that she had the catering manager cornered, she wasn't about to cut the woman loose until all doubts were exhausted.

"What about my getting locked in the storeroom?" she asked. "When you supposedly had a meeting...but didn't go to it?" She wondered if Connie would try to deny that.

"I went as far as the public phones, where I made a call to cancel a job interview at the last minute. I like working for Westbrook's, and I figured with Lamont Birch gone, I could keep my job without being blackmailed, so why shouldn't I?"

Though the photographs had proved to be a red herring, Pippa pressed her further. "And you didn't lock me in the storeroom?"

Connie gave her one of those looks. "Lock up the boss so I'd be fired for insubordination or something? Now you've got to be kidding."

She sounded so incredulous that Pippa believed her. "One last thing." One tiny doubt had been simmering. "Just before Lamont died, I stayed in the kitchen to replace those burned appetizers. Before you went upstairs, you sneaked something out of the refrigerator and onto your cart."

Connie flushed. "My stash."

"Drugs?"

"Chocolate. C'mon, I'll show you." Connie ducked into the kitchen, Pippa following. "It's kind of embarrassing. I'm diabetic, and every once in a while my blood sugar drops unexpectedly. A single piece of candy can even me out. The stress of that night was getting to me, I guess, so I took one upstairs just in case." Opening the refrigerator door, Connie picked up the non-descript white plastic bag Pippa had noticed but never had reason to check out. "Have one."

She looked inside. "Assorted chocolate candies." Not some deadly appetizer as she'd imagined. "All right. I give up. I'm satisfied."

"So I'm not fired?"

"You're not fired . . . and I won't share the information about your background with Lieutenant Jackson—or tell him Lamont was looking into it—unless he specifically asks." She was certain the detective would be delighted to make someone else sweat out his investigation.

"I appreciate that. Lamont Birch was something else," Connie said soberly. "I wonder how many other people he had the goods on. Maybe he picked on the wrong person, someone with a better motive and a shorter fuse."

MAYOR DARBY KEEGAN'S FUSE was getting shorter by the hour. He suspected, and he never sat still when he had misgivings—only a matter of time before he did something about them. Then it would be all over for her. . . .

Valerie Quinlan forced a smile for one of the catering staff as she checked out the private dining room, making certain everything was perfect. Only Keegan would have the bad taste to hold a luncheon the day after his murdered rival was buried so that he could exonerate himself to the media.

If only she could exonerate *herself*. If only she could go back in time and undo her stupidity.

Damn that film!

If only she'd gotten her hands on it. If only she hadn't given it to Lamont in the first place. If only... if only.

All the if onlys in the world weren't going to change her situation, Valerie thought grimly, staring over at the far corner of the room at the beautifully decorated Christmas tree, the most cherished symbol of the holiday that would never be the same for her. This one certainly had turned out to be plagued with crimson nightmares.

As she saw it, she had two choices. She could ride out the storm and hope she washed up as clean and bright as the angel topping the damned tree ... or, Valerie figured, her only other choice was to take action before it was too late.

"I'VE TAKEN ACTION, ordered the best of the force to investigate this unholy crime," Mayor Darby Keegan intoned in his speech preceding the free lunch that was doubtless the real reason the small private dining room was full. "We're gonna find the scum responsible..."

"Tell us something new," a reporter grumbled.

In the shadows at the rear of the room, Sky stood listening and watching. While the mayor droned on with the surface drivel they'd all heard before, the representatives of the media fiddled with their silverware, flirted with their water glasses, or sat looking just plain bored and hungry. Oddly enough, Gwen Walsh was there, appearing self-absorbed. Wondering what the mayor's aide was doing, he searched the room for Valerie Quinlan. She'd disappeared right after the old gasbag had approached the podium.

Sky looked toward the catering staff stationed near the exit to the warm-up kitchen. Standing at the back of the group with the manager, Pippa stood out from the rest, not only because she was one of the most beautiful women he'd ever seen, but also because she appeared to be the only observer in the room taking the mayor seriously. She focused on his every word, her lovely brow nettled, her lush mouth tense.

Undoubtedly Pippa feared she would be a scapegoat, medical examiner's report be damned, Sky thought. He wasn't about to let that happen. The least he could do, considering...

"Any questions?" the mayor asked.

Sky had scanned the clippings for hours that morning, but he hadn't been able to figure out why Birch had been collecting them. He didn't wait to be invited. Stepping out of the shadows, he spoke up loudly enough for everyone to hear.

"What did Lamont Birch know about you that you wanted to keep hidden?" Not that he thought he'd get a genuine answer. He just wanted to raise the question, shake up the gathering.

As the room lit up with response, Keegan flushed a deep red all the way to his receding hairline, making Sky think he was about to have an apoplectic fit. The mayor blustered a bit then practically shouted, "You gotta give Thornton here some slack—since he himself is under suspicion, he's desperate and lookin' for someone else to blame."

Tension hung in the air. Members of the media were no longer bored. They sat up, waiting, some rubbernecking in Sky's direction, prepared for a good fight.

And Sky was willing to give it to them. "The night Birch was murdered, he made some reference to you winding up with mud in your face—what did he mean by that?"

Now a loud murmur coursed through the room. Keegan boomed more loudly. "This man was not invited to chow down with us! Would someone *please* get him outta here!"

Having scored the point he'd come to make, Sky said, "I'll be happy to escort myself." He didn't want to force the duty on anyone else.

Reporters' questions to the mayor trailed after him.

"What *did* Lamont Birch mean by this mud reference?" one man reiterated.

"Did Birch have an objection to some specific project of yours?" asked a second.

A woman's voice rose above the others. "Your Honor, were you and Lamont Birch *deadly* enemies?"

No sooner had he traded the room for the carpeted area near the atrium than Pippa was at his side. "What was that all about? Do you think Keegan did it?" she demanded. "You found some answers in the folder, right? That's why you didn't wait to hear his responses to the reporters' questions!"

Lord, she was beautiful with her cheeks all flushed and her green eyes brilliant with anticipation. Sky regretted having to pop her balloon.

"Calm down," he said, taking her arm and moving her closer to the atrium where its nine-story Christmas tree was decorated with hundreds of ornaments and thousands of lights. Piped-in carols drifted up to them. "I didn't find anything. That's why I was trying to stir up the old gasbag."

Pippa gaped. Sky couldn't help himself. He tucked two fingers under her chin and gently closed her pretty mouth for her, then thought about opening it again in a far more personal way. Before he could follow through, she jerked her head and swiped at his hand.

"If you didn't find anything, Sky, then what was the point of making that fuss back there?"

"The point is, I was looking at those files with a foreign eye. I haven't been in this city for years, remember. I could have been looking straight at the seeds of a scandal and not even have recognized it."

"Hmm, I wonder if I would—"

"You can try tonight. At my place," he said, his reminder not so subtle. "In the meantime, I thought I'd try a little fishing expedition in hopes that Keegan might let something slip. I should have known he was too crafty to get caught with his pants down."

From the private dining room, one voice rose above the others—Keegan's, of course—though Sky couldn't make out the muffled words at this distance.

"If he needs to be caught at anything," Pippa said. "From the hubbub going on in there, looks like the mayor's luncheon got exactly the opposite results that he was hoping for." She hesitated a second before adding, "I only hope he deserves what he's getting."

"If Birch was keeping a file on him, he must have had reason. And if he were blackmailing His Honor, the Mayor..."

"But Keegan had people surrounding him all night," Pippa protested. "And I doubt Lamont would have taken anything from him. Not even a lousy canapé."

"He could have had an accomplice."

"Wasn't that supposed to be you?"

"I was never inside," he argued. "And I couldn't have been driving the sleigh and giving Birch the old heave-ho into the street at the same time. Therefore, the accomplice had to be someone else. Someone who would do whatever the mayor wanted, take orders, no questions asked."

"Valerie Quinlan?"

Exactly what he'd been thinking. "Keegan had her dogging me at the wake. She even suggested we get a cup of coffee. Maybe I should have accepted."

"Really?" Pippa sounded a tad stiff when she said, "So maybe we should take a harder look at the lovely Miss Quinlan."

He was looking hard at her. Her cheeks were pink, her eyes glittering, her hair fiery. "You wouldn't be jealous, would you?"

"Don't be ridiculous."

"Just a little?"

"You're imagining things."

"I'm flattered," he countered. "And liking it."

And liking her. Again Sky was tempted to kiss Pippa right there in public, mindless of the people walking by toward the elevators. He leaned in closer, but she flattened a hand smack in the middle of his chest.

"Don't even think about it," she warned him.

Mesmerized by her very touch—as rough as it was—Sky didn't budge. "Isn't that order against my constitutional rights?"

"You have no rights when it comes to me. No man does."

She sounded as if she never wanted one to have any again. Reminded of Dutch, Sky backed off. "We'll cram a look at the clippings somewhere into our evening," he said, staring down the atrium to a lower floor where he could swear he spotted Acacia Birch trying on a fur.

"Sounds like you have a lot planned. I need to be home at a decent hour. I'm a working girl, remember."

How could he forget?

Pippa McNabb was nothing Nola had told him to expect. She was hardworking, forthright, ambitious, honest... and the embodiment of the true, innocent image that had captivated him when he'd first seen her in the store window.

He, on the other hand, was a damned liar. Well, maybe not a liar exactly, but a perpetrator of fraud where she was concerned. And nothing, not even his growing feelings for her, could change what was.

"I'd better get back inside," Pippa said, indicating the private dining room.

He nodded curtly. "I'll pick you up here at your office, five-thirty sharp."

Anticipating their coming evening together with mixed feelings, Sky watched her go, his mood darkening.

DARKNESS SETTLED over the city early on this shortest day of the year. The sidewalk was slippery, and the cold and wet were definitely hard on the human foot, seeping in through leather as easily as if it were paper. And to top it off, carrying and keeping hidden a weighty burden added a degree of stress to the situation.

Couldn't stay in one spot too long or someone might notice. Trudge, trudge, trudge through the slush. Cross the alleyway, peek in discreetly in case anyone was there to see. No one at the car yet. It was parked right outside the security station. Impossible to get at. How many more passes would it take before she left the store?

A walk all the way to the corner relieved some pent-up energy. The walk back increased anticipation. What if, when she finally left the store, the McNabb woman wasn't alone?

Had to stop thinking like that. Had to believe this would all work out, that it would soon be over, that the next crime would go undetected until it was too late....

At the alley again. Spotting the redhead at last—and alone, thankfully—sent adrenaline surging. And prompted second thoughts. Pippa McNabb was no Lamont Birch. She wasn't even a bad sort, merely too nosy for her own good. She didn't deserve to be hurt again. But why did she have to interfere? Take what didn't belong to her?

That was a comforting thought. In her own way, the McNabb woman was a thief. Even from this distance it was evident she was stuffing her spoils into her purse.

Well, right back at her!

The crank of the engine was a warning signal to get into position. Since the alley beside Westbrook's was posted One Way, the McNabb woman would have to come past this spot.

The purring engine drew closer.

Hand tightening around the makeshift weapon, the attacker stepped directly into the path of the oncoming car.

Chapter Ten

The day had gone sour on Pippa. First there'd been the disappointment with the photo, then she'd returned to her office late only to discover various items out of place ... as if the room had been searched. And finally, Sky hadn't showed as promised.

Distracted, wondering if Sky had been the one digging around in her office, Pippa didn't see the pedestrian until it was almost too late. She stomped on the brake and brought the car to a squealing, lurching halt for the second time that day, stopping just a yard short of an accident. Heart thundering in her chest, she vowed to get a grip on herself before someone got hurt.

Needing a few seconds to catch her breath, Pippa waved on the pedestrian. She received her first shock of unease when the person stepped toward the car rather than moving on. The second shock hit her as she realized the person was wearing a long, hooded cape—dark green, if the alleyway's faint yellowish lights could be trusted.

Surely it couldn't be ... But spotting the sprig of withered mistletoe pinned just beneath the shoulder area, all doubts fled.

The pedestrian was wearing *her* cape, the stolen one, the one that had been spotted in the crowd behind Lamont right before he plunged off the curb.

The murderer! It had to be.

Eyes widening, Pippa strained to discern her attacker's identity even as the person approached the passenger side, right arm slowly rising. The answer to the mystery was hidden deep in the folds of the cape's full hood. Before Pippa could look more closely, the elevated arm shot downward, and before she could react, a brick in the gloved hand smashed into the windshield, fracturing it into a thousand tiny cracks.

Letting out a piercing scream of fright, she covered her face even as the windshield buckled and began to tumble inward in slow motion. She felt shards of the safety glass spill onto her. She then heard more breakage and peered out from beneath her protective arm just as the gloved hand tossed the brick onto the hood of the car and plunged inside the interior, making for the shoulder bag which she'd carelessly left on the passenger seat.

Pippa reacted blindly. Even as her attacker grabbed the bag, instinct pushed her to do the same. Four hands locked on the leather, the combatants engaged in a vicious tug-of-war, Pippa determined that this villain would not get away with one more crime if she could help it. "Let go!" she yelled, her fury heightening, giving her strength she'd never before called upon.

Her opponent was strong, far stronger than she. But like a terrier with a bone, Pippa hung on, refusing to give way, not even when the person continued the struggle one-handed, using the other to pound at Pippa's arms and wrists with a closed fist. Pippa shrieked, but more out of anger than from pain.

She noticed a passerby staring their way, though he didn't stop.

Having the advantage of strength, the attacker gained some territory. Lunging across the seats to take it back, Pippa renewed her grip even as her foot slipped off the brake. Still in drive, the car lurched slightly, then began creeping forward, barely missing another pedestrian—a small blonde, who, upon seeing the commotion, hurried on her way. But, thrown off balance, the attacker had to recoup. And Pippa spotted her chance.

Fixing her grip on the bag, she elbowed the horn to call attention to their struggle and began tapping first the accelerator, then the brake, so that the vehicle jerked forward a foot at a time, keeping her attacker at bay.

If only she didn't need both hands to keep a grip on her purse, she would be able to steer the car and run the villain down. Even while shocked by her violent imaginings, Pippa tapped the accelerator hard—the car nosed out over the sidewalk—then hit the brake harder and leaned into the horn. That's when her attacker freed one hand again, picked up the brick and aimed it at her head.

"There, see, her life is in danger!" came a woman's raised voice.

"Hey, whaddya think you're doin'?" a man bellowed.

The brick came smashing toward her. Pippa ducked, momentarily letting go of the bag, but the brick managed to clip her in the arm, anyway. Stunned, she gasped. Everything went slightly out of focus, and then she was seeing things: the hooded figure running, Sky jogging toward her.

The thrill of victory soared through Pippa, who threw her car into park and opened her door, yelling, "Don't let her get away!" But when Sky seemed more concerned with Pippa than the chase, the agony of defeat seared her. She crumpled against the car. "Damn!"

"What the hell was that all—"

"You okay, honey?" the woman's voice interrupted.

Pippa looked into the concerned expression of the blonde who'd passed by earlier and had obviously rounded up the militia. "Yes, thanks. This is a friend."

The man who'd come to her rescue muttered, "What a mess," after getting a closer look at the glass covering the inside of her car. "Ya want us to call the cops?"

"That won't be necessary," Sky said. He reached in and, with a gloved hand, brushed the broken glass from the driver's seat.

"I'll report the incident later," Pippa hedged. "Right now, I just want to go home."

"Yeah," the stranger said. "A smash and grab is small potatoes. Ya'd probably annoy the cops if ya dragged 'em out here."

She'd annoy them, all right, but for a reason very different from what he could guess. "Listen, I'd like to do something for you. A reward—"

"Hey, no need," the guy said, backing off. "Glad ta help."

When Pippa looked at the blonde, the woman shook her head. "I only hope someone would do the same for me if I'm ever in a tight spot."

Weakly, Pippa said, "Well, thanks again."

"Merry Christmas."

No sooner had the blonde turned away than Sky said, "If you're through with your moronic heroics, maybe you'll let me get you someplace comfortable."

She was too much in shock to rise to his bait. Maybe later. "Home."

"Fine. We'll go in my truck. C'mon, it's over here."

"What about my car?"

"I'll take care of it. Now let's see to you."

"My purse. I'm not going off without it after all that."

He scowled, but he ducked back inside her car. "Your stuff got dumped out," came his muffled voice.

Peering through the rear side window, she could see him gathering her things together and shoving them into her purse—until he got to the photographs, some of which had spilled from the envelope. He straightened and took a look before securing them and adding them to the bag.

"Your family?"

"Uh, not exactly." Unable to look at him, she ripped the purse out of his hands.

Silence. And then he said, "It can wait. Now let's get you into the Ranger." He helped her up into the high seat, his hand inadvertently coming into contact with her abused flesh and making her recoil. "You're hurt."

"It's nothing. My arm collided with a brick."

"You can still move it, can't you?"

She demonstrated. "Nothing broken. Just bruised and sore. And don't even think about suggesting an emergency room."

Shaking his head, he slammed the door and jogged over to her car, backed it down the alley and left it in one of the parking slots. Then, after going to the security entrance, he disappeared inside the store.

Pippa laid her head back, closed her eyes and took some deep breaths to calm herself. Several minutes passed before the other door opened.

"I alerted your security," Sky said, climbing in. "Older guy."

"Edgar Siefert."

"Here, take off your coat," he said, setting a resealable plastic bag filled with ice cubes on the dash. "This'll help keep the swelling and bruising down."

"I don't—"

"It's either a little self-help or the emergency room."

Grumbling, Pippa removed the coat, aware of his hands brushing her shoulders and back as he helped. Her left arm was definitely sore and quickly stiffening, and yet that didn't stop her physical reaction to Sky. Her breasts tightened as he gently touched her. He smoothed her coat over her shoulders and, beneath the thick material, set the bag of ice on the sore spot. Then he placed her gloved right hand over the ice and pulled the lapels of her coat as close together as he could.

"Warm enough?" he asked.

"Yes. Satisfied?" she countered.

"I'll let you know when," Sky said provocatively, and tucked the coat's collar close to her neck, trailing his fingers over her flesh. Then he started the Ranger. "I left your car keys with Siefert." Pulling the four-wheeler onto the street, he headed west. "He'll get the windshield taken care of. I told him we'd take care of the police."

"Why bother? They won't believe me. At least Jackson won't."

"What's Jackson got to do with a smash and grab?"

"Something, I would hope, since this was no ordinary theft attempt." She took a big breath. "I believe I've met our murderer."

"What! Who?"

"Good question. I didn't see a face."

"If you didn't have the opportunity to recognize anyone, what makes you think the person who attacked you was the same person who murdered Birch?"

"Remember the missing hooded green cape?"

"The attacker was wearing a cape." Sky jerked them to a stop at a red light. "You're certain it was *your* cape?"

"I pinned a fresh sprig of mistletoe to the left shoulder the night of the fund-raiser. It was dried up, but it was still there."

"Good God, why didn't you say something?"

"I did. I believe I said, 'Don't let her get away.' You ignored me," she said, bitterly disappointed that he had another thing in common with Dutch.

"I was concerned that you might be hurt." Sky stated. "There's a difference." A moment's silence and then, driving off when the light changed to green, he picked up on Pippa's reproof. "*Her.* You said *her*—"

"An assumption because of the cape," Pippa grumbled. "I have no way of knowing for certain. Man or woman, that person is stronger than I am."

"That's not saying much." She gave him a dirty look. Though he didn't glance her way, he said, "I felt that," as if he had eyes on the side of his head. "So tell me I'm wrong. Tell me you can bench press your weight."

"I've never had occasion to try. Nor the need. Nor the desire. Until today, I was perfectly satisfied being a hundred-and-twenty-pound weakling."

"You did pretty good for a weakling."

"Is that praise I hear?"

"From my lips to yours."

That conjured up a vision that made her squirm in her seat. She could almost feel that kiss....

But when he asked, "Wait a minute. Why would a murderer be so concerned about stealing your purse?" her discomfort took a new turn.

"I'm not a mind reader," she said, unable to keep the tension out of her voice. What *had* the murderer been after? she wondered. Surely not the photographs that had proved to be a dead end. But what else could it be?

"You must have some idea," Sky insisted.

"Not exactly," Pippa hedged. And then, realizing he was turning onto the Kennedy Expressway, she was delighted to have reason to distract him. "Wait a minute. You're going out of the way to get me home. You should have taken Lake Shore Drive."

"Not to get to *my* home."

"Your—"

"We had a date, remember."

"But—"

"And you can't very well kick me out of my own home if you don't like something I say or do."

That gave her pause. "Exactly what are you planning to do?"

"See to that arm, for one."

"I didn't know you were a professional."

"I told you I'm an expert in survival skills," Sky reminded her. "That includes first aid, CPR, and the Heimlich manuever. Bruised arms are small potatoes," he added, his words mimicking those of the stranger who'd been kind enough to come to her rescue.

She didn't really want to argue. And though she wanted to say she could take care of herself, the idea of being taken care of *by him* sounded kind of nice. "Just don't get any ideas," she muttered.

"Too late."

Pippa's cheeks grew warm at the implication.

They had been driving for several minutes, long enough for tension to start rebuilding in Pippa, when Sky said, "You should remove the ice pack for twenty to thirty minutes, then use it again."

Doing as he suggested, she wrapped the plastic bag in her thick woolen scarf and set it in the back away from the heater's vents. Many of the ice cubes were already starting to melt from her body warmth, but some would undoubtedly survive the trip.

"Half an hour," she mused. "We'll still be driving?"

"My place is a ways out. An unincorporated area near Half Day."

"That is quite far. How did you find it?"

"My father signed it over to me when his wife prodded him into retiring to California. Since it would have been mine someday, he chose to give it to me now."

Which meant his father must be set comfortably or he wouldn't have been able to afford such a generous gesture. The main reason she was glad to have inherited the store was that it ensured her parents' comfortable future—not that her brothers weren't equally concerned.

Sky interrupted her musing. "My turn."

"For what?"

"Questions. Specifically... if those photographs aren't of your family, then who?"

"I don't know."

"You always carry around photographs of strangers?"

Caught in a tough bind, she had to give him at least part of the truth. "It was that film I found in the store. You saw it, remember?"

"I assumed you were the one who'd dropped the film in the first place. You had someone else's film developed?" He sounded incredulous. "Why?"

"To see if I could figure out who it belonged to." *Silence.* He was waiting. She swallowed and said, "All right, all right, I, uh, thought maybe the murderer had dropped it," and hoped he would leave it at that.

"The murderer," he echoed, his voice tight. "And what brought you to that conclusion?"

Quickly, she told him about remembering Lamont's argument, about hearing something hitting the floor, about later finding the film and about hoping the photographs would finger the murderer.

"And you didn't say a word about it to me. Your supposed partner."

"Well, uh, I thought I'd take a look at the photographs first." Certain he knew she was hedging again, Pippa grew defensive. "I didn't get them back until this morning."

"But you saw me early this afternoon."

"By then I realized it was all a mistake, that someone playing tourist lost the film."

"That still doesn't explain why you wouldn't have told me about it, not unless..."

He didn't finish the statement; she refused to. How could she tell him she hadn't trusted him, that she had suspected the photographs might implicate *him?* How could he not know?

More than an uncomfortable minute went by before he said, "So I wasn't the only one who knew you found the film. The photographs must be the reason you were attacked tonight."

Sky sounded as if he was speaking through clenched teeth. Pippa couldn't blame him. She thought of apologizing, then figured she'd better leave it alone. "It seems like that ought to be the answer," she said instead, "but the pictures don't prove out that theory."

"Then what was the attacker after?"

"My shoulder bag."

"Why?" he persisted.

"I don't know!"

"Looks like we have a lot more work ahead of us tonight than I'd counted on," Sky muttered. "First the clippings. Now the photographs."

"I could study them until I was blue in the face and not get anything more sinister out of that packet than a record of a family outing."

Frustrated, Pippa heaved a sigh and tried to make herself more comfortable. She succeeded only in irritating her arm. Expecting Sky to continue the argument, she was pleased when he left it alone. Resting her head against the seat back and closing her eyes, she felt herself drifting. Sky didn't bother her until it came time for another application of the ice pack. This time, she managed it herself.

Thankfully, by the time Sky left the expressway, the tension had left the vehicle. And when he turned off the main road, she was looking forward to seeing where he lived.

"A couple more minutes."

Minutes that they traveled in near dark, for no streetlights lit their way. Talk about being in the boonies. Even so, the moon glowed blue-white off the snow, and she could see that fields surrounded them. And powerful animals that kicked up a spray of white skittered across the pasture.

"Horse country," she murmured.

"What's left of it."

"Looks like they more than tolerate you."

"Yeah, well, to them I'm Dad or something." He sounded almost embarrassed. "I hand raised a few of them myself. The others I've had since they were juveniles. I figured it'd be best to get hold of them while they were young so I could raise them right."

Like kids, she thought, touched that he was so gentle with beasts that weighed more than she did—somewhere around one hundred and fifty to two hundred pounds, she guessed. But then, Sky had been mostly gentle with her, despite the way they'd started off on a bad footing. His attitude had done a three-sixty since they'd met. She remembered being certain he didn't like her even though he didn't know her…and that from the first he seemed to know more than was comfortable about her.

Sky slipped both hands into his pockets, then held them out. The beasts vied for the lumps, which looked suspiciously like sugar cubes, sitting in his palms.

"Bribes?"

"Treats."

Amazed by their interaction, she said, "I always thought reindeer were actually wild."

"You're thinking of their larger cousins, the Woodlands caribou found in Alaska. These are Greenland caribou and have been domesticated by the Laplanders for centuries. In northern Europe, they're considered beasts of burden and their job is to pull sleds through the tundra."

"Then how did your reindeer end up in Alaska?"

"Actually, all of these guys come from Alaskan racing stock."

"Like horses again."

He laughed. "As light as you are, I don't think they'd want you on their backs. More like sled dogs." He made one more foray into his pockets, saying, "All right, guys, this is it. I should say that they're not all guys. Dancer, Prancer, Vixen and Cupid are females."

Again she registered surprise, since she hadn't known both male and female reindeer had antlers. But then, it was a night for surprises.

Hopefully, all the bad ones were out of the way.

Sky's putting his arm around her shoulders to lead her to the house definitely felt good. Her blood pulsed so that she felt vitally alive, ready for anything. A glow of anticipation invigorated her. For the first time in a year, she chose to stop listening to the instinct that fought her letting another man get too close. She wanted to be close to Schuyler Thornton, naturalist and survival-skills expert.

Despite all her minor comparisons over the past few days, Sky was nothing like Dutch Vanleer, football player, department store magnate...cheat and liar.

"We can go in through the conservatory," he said, leading her along a path to a protrusion of leaded-glass windows, which were filled with plants.

"Mmm, wonderful," she murmured, breathing in the smell of the damp soil and clean air of the green room as they entered.

She was further delighted by the house's interior. Though the place had seen better days, and, in addition to the structural repairs that were being made on the outside, could use a loving hand not only to spruce it up but modernize it a bit, the heart of the house was magical. Both the living and dining rooms were wood paneled and beamed, having brick fireplaces with openings wide enough to lie down in and intricately designed brass chandeliers sturdy enough to swing from.

She wandered to the central hall between the two rooms, where a giant Christmas tree had been put up, and she drank in every detail. "It reminds me of a European hunting lodge."

"Too big and dark?" Sky was beside her, taking her shoulder bag, helping her off with her coat.

Again the thrills his touch brought assaulted her. "Fanciful," she countered. "A setting for a fairy tale."

Or a romance.

After he'd checked on her bruised arm, which was feeling amazingly better, they ate in the sunken dining room—not at the main table that seated an even dozen, but at a more intimate, hand-carved one set in front of a roaring fire that Sky had prepared ahead of time. He'd also asked the woman who did his cleaning to prepare dinner, and what she had left for them was a feast. Stuffed chicken, whipped squash, oven-browned potatoes and a dish of hearty spiced cranberries.

"There's enough food here for an entire family," she said. "So tell me about yours."

He didn't look up from his food. "The reindeer are pretty much it."

"Oh, come on. You have parents, don't you? Didn't you say they just recently gave you this place?"

"My father did. When I was a kid, my parents divorced and remarried."

Right. She remembered his saying his father's wife had wanted him to move to California.... "So is this place yours alone or do you have to share it with siblings?"

"I don't have any siblings."

That was jarring to a woman with four. "None?"

"I did have an older brother, but we were estranged years ago..." He hesitated, then finished, "After he stole my college sweetheart. I was planning on bringing Vanessa into the family... not sharing her with other family members."

"He married her?"

"No. He used and discarded her as he did most women. Eventually he married one, who was far nicer, even more innocent of his true nature."

The way he was looking at her... She concentrated on her food, moving it around the plate with her fork, taking a bite that seemed oddly difficult to swallow.

"How awful that must have been for you," she finally said. "So what happened after you found out what your brother did?"

"We had a knock-down-and-drag-out fight. He was bigger. Stronger. But I was angrier and had something to prove. He got the worse end of the deal. He didn't like that. Afterward, we were each glad to disown the other. I never spoke to him or heard from him again."

His voice was emotionless as though he had schooled himself into not caring. But Pippa saw through the facade. No matter what had happened between the brothers, Sky cared. She reached out and covered his hand with hers. "And you've never made peace with each other?"

"You could say that."

His response was as odd as his tone. But considering how touchy he was about the subject—and rightfully so—Pippa didn't press the issue.

So she was surprised when Sky added, "I'd like to find a way to forgive him, but I haven't been able to. Being saddled with this hatred is like a festering sore.

You never heal, and I don't want to be sick inside forever."

"What would he have to do to earn your forgiveness?"

"An apology would go a long way. He never once said he was sorry."

"Maybe he will…if you believe hard enough that it's possible."

"You know what I really believe? That it's too late."

Sad. But Pippa could understand why he felt that way. He'd said college sweetheart. Staring at his handsome face brushed with strokes of his dark hair, she guessed Sky was in his early thirties. That meant he'd been carrying around this burden for a decade.

Swallowing her mouthful of food hard, she asked, "You still love her?"

"No. I don't have room in my heart for her—or for hatred—anymore."

"That's good. Forgiveness is its own reward," she said, repeating something her mother had often told her children when they were angry either with each other or with outsiders.

"I wonder if you really believe that," Sky said. "Or if push came to shove, you'd be like the rest of us."

Instincts on alert, Pippa had the feeling that Sky had done something he wanted her to forgive him for. But what? For being rude? Pushy? Aggravating?

Or was there something darker in his soul that was bothering him?

Chapter Eleven

Sky's very soul was burdened with the way he'd been deceiving Pippa. And for a moment, he thought he might confess all, believing that she meant what she said about forgiveness being its own reward. He opened his mouth. He wanted to say the words. But the words wouldn't come.

Instead he changed the subject. Eyeing the crumbs of food left on her plate, he asked, "Have room for dessert?"

"Not now, thanks. But—"

"Then why don't we move into the living room," he suggested. "We've got some work to do."

Pippa seemed disappointed...and somehow disturbed. He feared her instincts were aroused and that she would be determined to get the truth out of him. And so he was relieved when her intent expression relaxed.

"You're right. We have a full evening ahead of us."

He only wished he could add *night* to that.

Before getting down to work, Pippa insisted on refrigerating leftovers and stacking dishes on the kitchen counter, despite Sky's insistence that his cleaning woman would take care of everything in the morning.

Then he started a blaze in the living-room fireplace. The hand-carved wooden mantel was decorated with fat red candles and fresh holly, compliments of his cleaning woman. And rather than having them sit opposite each other on sofas, Sky forced more intimacy than Pippa probably wanted by moving several floor pillows directly in front of the hearth.

Fetching the crammed file that had meant next to nothing to him, he realized she was standing there, staring at the romantic seating arrangement. "Curling up near the fireplace will be cozy."

"That's what I'm afraid of," she murmured.

"We'll have to get close to work efficiently."

She raised her eyebrows but dropped to the small area rug warmed by the fire and leaned an elbow against one of the floor pillows. Wearing a blush pink angora sweater, her flame red hair fluffed out around her shoulders, she was a portrait of heavenly beauty. Cozying up next to her, the Keegan folder the only thing separating them, Sky could well imagine he'd died and gone to heaven.

His senses filling with her, Sky handed Pippa the folder and forced himself to the serious subject at hand. "I've given it my best shot but haven't been able to make anything of the contents."

"Give me a few minutes. . . ."

Grateful for the opportunity to enjoy her presence fully, Sky leaned back and watched Pippa, aware of every gesture, every nuance of movement, as she paged through the clippings. At first she appeared self-conscious, but eventually she seemed to forget he was there and concentrated on her task. He mentally photographed her every expression. The way her brow nettled and the way the delicate skin around her eyes crinkled. The way her lips quirked and the way her nose twitched. Besotted fool that he was, he couldn't get enough of her. And so he was disappointed when she looked up from her perusal.

"Let's be logical about this," she suggested. "Why would Lamont keep clippings of everyday happenings?"

"Birch must have been looking for a reason to get on Keegan's case politically, to give himself the edge in this so-called run for the mayoral election. So he needed to document Keegan's every move."

"The mayor has always been irritating, but his activities are mostly harmless." Pippa spread out several of the last entries in the folder. "Speeches at city council meetings, appearances at museum openings, things like that we can eliminate. The only two items that raised any real commotion that I can remember were Keegan's insistence on bringing casinos into Chicago—which he still hasn't given up on—and his support of the City Streets Complex."

Scooting over even closer to Pippa, Sky took a better look at the newspaper items in question. "I can understand objections to the casinos. People are always afraid of organized crime getting a new foothold in the city." Breathing in her scent, he was slightly distracted from the shot of the mayor driving a shovel into the earth at a ground breaking. "But what's the big deal about a new housing complex?"

"It was controversial because the land is directly west of the downtown area."

Noting the city skyline behind Keegan, Sky said, "I can see that. Prime real estate."

Sky transferred his attention to Pippa, a spectacular view as far as he was concerned. But he was obviously making her nervous.

For her voice quivered just a tad when she said, "Land that housing projects were built on more than twenty years ago. The projects became so run-down that a lot of apartments became unlivable." She shifted away from him slightly, giving herself more breathing room. "Next thing we knew, tenants were being moved around to fill vacancies in some buildings, while the then empty buildings were scheduled for demolition."

"And instead of rebuilding better living quarters for the poor, City Streets is intended for those in the middle-to-upper income brackets."

"Exactly."

"Somehow," he said, hooking a red curl with one finger, "I think you've got it."

"But what?" She swatted at his hand as if he were a pesky fly. "Keegan was never accused of doing anything illegal."

"Maybe he took some under-the-table money for the dealings."

She hunched over the folder and away from him. "Nothing in here indicates that. We're stopped cold."

"It doesn't seem to me that a man like Birch would keep his schemes to himself," Sky said, removing the folder from her grasp and setting it safely on the side of the cushions away from the fire. "I'll bet *someone* knows where he planned to go from there."

"Who?"

"Possibly the grieving widow."

"Well, then," Pippa said, sounding too relieved to be flattering, "another surprise visit to Acacia is in order."

When she tried to rise, Sky clamped a hand around her good arm. "I hope you don't mean tonight. Tonight I want to be alone with you."

She flushed and settled back down. "We should really look at the photographs to see if I missed something."

"Let's take a break first. I'll pour us some brandy—to aid digestion," he said, giving her an excuse to accept. "And you can tell me about *your* family and what you all do for the holidays."

"A *small* brandy."

Smothering a grin at the minor victory, he leaped to his feet and made for an antique, hinged writing desk that he was using as a liquor cabinet. "So, tell me."

"Traditionally we all spend the holidays together. Eating, drinking, singing Christmas carols, opening presents. The usual."

Not usual for him—he was lucky if he spent the holidays with a couple of friends—though Sky had to admit he'd be willing to give the experience a chance with someone he cared about. Pouring generous splashes of the brandy into two glasses, he said, "Define *we.*"

"Mom, Dad, my four brothers, now two sisters-in-law—Shelby's a new addition—" she clarified, "a niece and a nephew and me. So far."

He said, "So you're not the only unmarried McNabb sibling," before he realized he'd gone straight to the topic he'd wanted to avoid.

"Only one of my brothers is a confirmed bachelor. Another's marriage was annulled."

Thankful she'd skipped over her own widowhood, Sky put a sprig of mistletoe—which also must have been left by the cleaning woman—into his pocket and rejoined Pippa. The crackling fire was nice and toasty.

Handing her a drink, he said, "Skoal," then clinked his glass to hers and took a sip as did she. "When you say holidays, do you mean Christmas Eve or Day?"

"The whole magilla, as Pop would say," Pippa told him with a huge grin that was so irresistible it warmed him inside. "We always gather by the fire after Christmas Eve dinner and light a Yule log."

"Isn't that some kind of pagan ritual, to celebrate the rebirth of the sun?"

"Probably. But like the original ornamental trees and Father Christmas, who went through several reincarnations before he became Santa Claus, the Yule log has become part of our modern Christian tradition."

"Which is?"

"While we burn a big log, each of us makes a list of our most cherished wishes for the coming year. Then we fold up our lists and throw them into the fire in hopes that our wishes will come true."

She sipped at her brandy and breathed out through pursed lips as if releasing fire. Pursed as if asking for a kiss... And Sky was oh so tempted to lean over and capture her heat. His lips already burned for thinking about it.

"Oh, and part of the tradition is saving a piece of the charred log to start the next year's fire," she went on, breaking the suspended moment. "Supposedly the kindling is magical and will protect your home from fire, flood and lightning for a whole year."

"Not a bad Christmas wish in itself." Sky had only one wish for himself... a wish that would never be fulfilled. For obvious reasons, he would never have Pippa's heart. "Then what?"

"Then we all go to sleep and wait for Christmas morning when we can open the gifts."

"Your parents must have a pretty big house to sleep so many people."

"My unmarried brothers and I set out sleeping bags in front of the fireplace. It's nice and cozy and reminds me of when we were kids."

"And you don't get on each other's nerves?"

"Is that what people do to you? Is that why you prejudge them?"

Fearing they were entering dangerous waters once more, Sky ignored her questions and pulled out the sprig of mistletoe. Twirling it between two fingers, enjoying the blush he brought to her cheeks, he said, "Did you know this baby was the most sacred plant of the Druids? It grew on the oak tree and remained green in winter when the oak shed its leaves. Ancient peoples believed that mistletoe held the oak tree's soul safe during what they thought of as its winter death." He twirled the sprig again and moved it closer to her face. "And so it was also believed that a kiss under its glistening berries was a guarantee of a fruitful union."

Pippa sat frozen, unable to take her eyes off the small green sprig.

Sky continued moving his hand oh so slowly above her head, moving his face oh so gradually toward hers, giving Pippa every chance in the world to object or to move away. As if she were hypnotized, her eyes fluttered and closed to slits. Her breathing quickened. Her tongue darted out to moisten her lips.

If she wasn't offering an invitation...

Tucking the sprig of mistletoe in her hair, admiring the green against the fire red curls, he took her up on the offer. He closed his mouth over hers and watched her lids flutter yet again before squeezing shut.

When his tongue slid inside her, Pippa's good arm snaked around his neck. The bruised one lay cradled in the small opening that still existed between them. She flattened that palm against his chest, her fingernails tangling in the cables of his sweater. He could feel every subtle motion, was aroused by the small sounds trapped at the back of her throat.

He made sounds, too. Groans that welled up from deep within him. He'd made love to several women over the years since Vanessa had betrayed him, but none that he'd loved as well—certainly not better—until now. No other woman he had ever known was worthy to be compared to Pippa McNabb.

He let his hand stray down her back to find the bottom edge of her sweater. The need to feel her skin against his palm grew with every inch. The need to love her and have her love him was even stronger. The knowledge that that could never be almost stopped him.

Almost...

"Pippa," he murmured against her mouth when he slipped his hand under the sweater.

In answer, she arched her back so he could more easily slide his hand around to her breast. The bra she wore was a thin confection, no barrier to his quest. When he cupped her and rubbed the nipple with his thumb, she sighed deeply into his mouth. Her fingers curled in the long hair at the back of his neck and she kissed him harder, with the same impatience he himself was feeling.

He quickly shot around to her back and undid the bra, traversed the opposite direction more slowly and this time beneath the gossamer material. Before he knew what was happening, he was removing her sweater, breaking the kiss so he could find and pebble her nipples with his lips and teeth.

And all the while, part of him knew that he shouldn't be doing this—not when he really cared for her.

Guilt slowed him. He was breathing heavily. Trying to do the right thing before it was too late, before blind passion took him over the edge.

"Don't stop, please," she whispered, now using both hands to press his face to her breast. "I want you like I've never wanted anyone...."

With those words, he was lost.

LOST IN PASSION, PIPPA pushed everything away but the present. Helping Sky remove her sweater and bra, she didn't want to think about past mistakes or murder investigations. She only wanted to concentrate on the man who held her and the wonderful sensations he was creating in her body, which had waited so long for his singular touch....

Oddly, she felt as if she knew Sky. *Really* knew him. That they'd only met days ago seemed laughable when he was already a part of her.

She smoothed a hand up his cheek, looked into those blue, blue eyes and sighed deeply.

"What?"

"I don't know why I've been fighting it," she murmured, feeling wanton in his arms and loving every second of it. Who cared that she lay there half-naked when the day before she'd still been mistrusting him? When something was right between two people, it was right.

His brow furrowed. "Maybe we shouldn't—"

She stopped him by placing her hand over his mouth. "Traditionally, it's supposed to be the woman doing the protesting, the man reassuring her. You're going to give me a complex." He cupped her hand with his and edged it up so he could fully kiss her palm. Threads of desire ran through her veins straight to her feminine center.

"Heaven forbid. I don't want to give you anything but your most cherished wishes," he said. "And I don't want to be something you regret tomorrow."

Reminded of their earlier discussion, she whispered, "You would be on my Yule log list, so how could I regret you tomorrow?"

He groaned and adjusted position so that she lay under him against several stacked floor pillows. Murmuring, "I knew you were an angel the first time I saw you," he spread out her hair around her. Then his lips found better work than talking. They feathered her hairline... her eyes... her nose... her mouth.

Finally kissing her deeply, passionately, Sky shifted so that she could feel the full length of his desire pressed against her thigh. Wanting him to explore the depth of hers, she began undoing his belt and waistband. He struggled with his sweater, letting go of her lips only when forced to it, so that he could bring the knit over his head.

They became abandoned as they stripped, throwing clothes to every corner of the room. It became a game, two adults for a few minutes reliving young adulthood. Only Pippa didn't think she'd ever been so carefree with Dutch, the only other man she'd ever slept with.

Lighthearted and loving every second of her growing anticipation, Pippa was laughing when Sky, glorious in his nudity, knelt over her, his features serious.

She reached up for him. His eyes closed and she knew that she'd been looking forward to this since the moment they'd met. Holding her breath, she waited for him to come to her. And when he did, she knew heaven, experiencing only the tiniest of hesitations when she accidently hit her sore arm.

Though she bit back her moan of pain, the ringing sensation reminded Pippa that she had more to occupy her than their lovemaking. The investigation was no longer a game. Not when someone had intentionally hurt her. And try as she would, she couldn't put it out of mind. What would come next? Another dead body? Hers?

Somehow the thought only made her lovemaking more urgent—kisses deeper, strokes faster, climax more thrilling.

For when matching wits with a murderer, who could count on saving any tomorrows for regrets?

PIPPA REGRETTED FALLING asleep without any covers on, that was for certain. Waking stiff and chilled, she snuggled closer to her only heat source—Sky—and fought the daylight that crept into the room.

Daylight?

Oh, no!

She had to get to Westbrook's before Rand found out about the incident in her car. She had no doubts her brother would panic when she didn't answer her home phone. He'd definitely initiate a three-state search for her.

Choosing to retain some modesty, she didn't wake Sky immediately, but slipped out of his arms to start a search for her clothes. Her sweater was closest. Bra-less, she slipped into the angora to chase away the chill. Her bikini bottoms decorated a bowl of fruit sitting on a nearby table. After climbing into them, she grabbed an apple and began munching, even though Sky had gone for their dessert in the middle of the night.

Remembering how they'd satiated their appetites first with chocolate mousse-filled cream puffs, then with each other, she immediately grew warm enough all the way to her toes.

Remembering also brought a grin to her lips. She was happy. Really happy for the first time in . . . she didn't know how long. Years, maybe. She had been happy with Dutch for a while, but that had been so long ago.

When she slipped into her slacks, she did an imitation of Connie, singsonging her mother's favorite irritating early morning refrain. "Rise and shine. Rise and shine. Time to get up, lazybones."

Sky merely rolled over, facedown into the pillows, and grunted something unintelligible.

"You just want me to do all the work," she said, picking up his sweater and flinging it at him.

She found one of his socks—that went sailing across the room next—then one of hers. Hopping, she pulled it on. One foot covered, the other bare, she approached Sky's jeans, gave him a glance, and wondered if she really wanted him to cover those magnificent buns. Humorously thinking they would get frostbitten if he didn't, she grabbed up the jeans, only to have his pockets empty out on her.

"Rats!"

A muffled "What?" came from the pillows before the fireplace.

"I dumped everything," she said, squatting to scoop up loose change, a key ring and his wallet.

The leather shifted and some of the contents spilled out of that, too. Dropping everything else on his jeans, she knelt and patiently gathered up some loose pieces of paper that had been in his wallet, glancing at them out of sheer curiosity.

Receipts, notes to himself . . . and a photograph.

Why would a man who denied family ties have what was so obviously a family photo in his wallet?

Taking a better look at the shot, she froze. Grinning up at her were a woman and two boys with arms slung around each other's shoulders. One boy was about eight or nine, the other perhaps twelve or thirteen.

Unless she was mistaken, the woman was a much younger version of Nola Yarbrough—only she hadn't been a Yarbrough at the time. That was her current husband's name. Vanleer had been her first husband's. And the older boy was definitely Nola's son, Dutch.

Heart pounding, Pippa stared into the youthful face of her late husband. In shock, not wanting to make the obvious connection, she plopped her bottom on the floor and tried to find some other explanation. Only she couldn't.

"Hey, what's going on over there?" croaked a raspy voice that belonged to a man she didn't know, after all.

"You tell me," she said softly, tears suddenly blurring the two boys who had only a passing resemblance.

"I'm hungry. How about you?" Sky asked, his voice growing stronger as sounds from his direction told Pippa he was rising and dressing.

The similarity was in their mouths, in the way the lips curled into a smile . . . the very same smile she had recognized on Sky the first time she'd spotted it. Dear God, she'd known there was something familiar about him. Why couldn't she have figured out what?

"Hey, what's up?" Sky asked.

She looked at him blankly. He was wearing his sweater, Jockey shorts and one sock. His dark hair was all tangled. She supposed she was responsible for that. And for the expression that suddenly stiffened his features into the face of a stranger when he got a look at the object in her hand.

"I can explain. . . ."

He *was* a stranger to her. "Can you?" Dead. As dead as Dutch was. And that broke her heart in a way her late husband had never been able to do. "I'm all ears."

He stared into eyes that were even now filling with the proof of her grief. "I'm sorry."

"For what? For not telling me you were Dutch's brother? Or for getting caught in your lie?"

"Half brother. My father was Nola's second husband. And I never exactly lied to you."

"Don't you dare try to split hairs here! You knew who I was all along. I couldn't figure out why. I wondered how you could know certain things about me. Like that crack about quarterbacks. What was that?" She choked back a sob, but she couldn't stop the tears from rolling down her cheeks. "Revenge? Is that what this is all about—some sick plot to get revenge because your brother died and I didn't?"

"No!" He loomed over her, his pose as threatening as any of Dutch's had been in those last dark months of their marriage. As if he realized he was frightening her, Sky backed off and said, "I swear."

Hating her own weakness—realizing that she'd fallen for another man unworthy of her love, another man who thought she wasn't worthy of his respect—Pippa scrambled to her feet. "Then why the hell didn't you tell me who you were?"

"I had my reasons."

"I guess you did." Obviously, ones he didn't mean to share with her. "Whatever they were, you must be enjoying yourself. You fooled me. You used me. You're no better than your brother!''

Throwing down the photograph, she spun around, wildly looking for her missing sock. He stopped her cold, his hand holding her as if she were of no consequence.

The same way Dutch had . . .

Fury blinding her and coloring the picture before her red, she struck out as hard as she could. As if watching a slow-motion scene from afar, she saw her hand connect with Sky's face. Felt his jerked reaction. Saw the darkness veil his face. "Let go of me!" she screamed, punctuating the words by striking out at him again and again.

Before he could hit her?

But when Sky released her, he made no threatening move. He simply stood there, looking like a man who'd gambled everything and lost.

But what had he lost? He'd been the one holding all the cards. He'd known exactly who she was, while she'd stupidly fallen in love with him.

With Dutch's brother!

This crimson nightmare was never going to end.

Chapter Twelve

"You ruined it," she whispered, sobbing freely now. "But there never really was a chance for us, was there?"

His face etched in something akin to despair, he shook his head. "I'm sorry," he said again.

An apology she didn't think she would ever accept. "Then why?" Why couldn't he just have let her be?

"I couldn't help myself. It's my only defense."

A weak defense at best. Pippa wiped the tears from her eyes. Silently she rounded up her other sock, her shoes, her coat, hat, gloves and shoulder bag. Only when she was fully dressed and ready to leave did she realize she couldn't. Not when her late husband's brother had the only means of transportation on the place.

Luckily, he was dressed and prepared to leave. "C'mon. I'll take you home."

"To Westbrook's."

Silently she led the way to the Ranger, her eyes straying everywhere, staying away from him. She caught sight of the reindeer, several of whom wandered over to the fence, their noses pressed between the split rails as if they were looking for another dose of affection from Sky—something she would never again experience. Her heart went out to them because she couldn't tolerate feeling sorry for herself.

And as she got into the passenger seat, she thought about the love and trust those reindeer had for this human who had betrayed her. She'd counted Sky's unusual relationship with the reindeer in his favor, thinking he had to be a good person. How could she have been so completely fooled?

It wasn't until they were halfway to the city when the traffic got heavier, that she figured her emotions were under control. "Are you going to tell me why you sought me out in the first place?"

"I had to get to know you."

"Because I was the wife of the brother you disowned ten years ago?" At least a year before she'd met Dutch, who never had mentioned any sibling.

"In a way, yes."

"In what way?" she persisted.

"I was doing it for Nola."

"Now it's coming clear. Nola never did like me. I stole her precious son. Of course she had another son, not that she ever mentioned *you*," she said, realizing she was being purposely cruel.

But if the knowledge bothered Sky, he didn't let on. He sounded resigned when he said, "Nola blamed me for the split. Said a woman wasn't worth shaking up the family for. Vanessa *wasn't*," he added, as if some other woman might be. "But it was the principle of the thing."

"And after Dutch died, Nola was like a woman demented, said I shouldn't have anything that belonged to her son because I'd meant to divorce him," Pippa remembered aloud. "She said it was too bad he died before that happened. She also said Dutch changed his will . . . but he hadn't.''

"Are you certain?"

The real truth started to gel for her. "Is that it? You believe Nola? When our lawyer couldn't produce a new will, your mother accused me of hiding this nonexistent document. Believe me, I did look for it.''

"Since you were still married, a new will wouldn't have kept you from inheriting half of Dutch's estate, anyway. In Illinois, you're automatically entitled.''

"So Nola convinced you I was greedy and manipulative without our having even met." Sky's silence and the way his hands gripped the steering wheel told Pippa that she'd hit a nerve. Did he really think she was so enamored of possessions? "I didn't care about the money. What other garbage did your mother fill your head with?"

"She told me Dutch had been sorry about our separation for a long, long time, only he was too proud to be the first one to make a move at reconciliation. I didn't believe her at first. I fought coming home, but then Nola said she could prove it. She said Dutch made me the main beneficiary in the new will, and that he wouldn't have done that unless he'd wanted to put our differences in the past. In some way, I'd hoped to regain the brother I'd lost, even if he was dead.''

"Why didn't you just tell me the truth?" she asked, sad for herself. Sad for him. If he thought Dutch had remorse for the despicable things he'd done . . . then Sky had known a different man than she had. "Why did you have to lie just like your brother?''

"I'm nothing like Dutch!"

"But you are, more than you realize. If you had come to me in honesty, we could have saved ourselves a lot of grief." At least she could have. Then something else occurred to her. "When I found you in his study…you were looking for the will, weren't you?"

He took a deep breath. "Guilty as charged. Can you ever forgive me?"

She thought about it for a moment. Could she? Did she want to? To be honest, part of her did. But an even bigger part kept her on edge, kept her wondering if this was part of Sky's ploy to get what he wanted…whatever that might be. Obviously, she couldn't tell the truth from a lie anymore. And look where it had gotten her— feeling used and brokenhearted.

"I can't believe you could make love to me with such distrust and so many lies between us," she said firmly. "No, I don't see how I can forgive you."

And then he reminded her, "I thought you believed forgiveness was its own reward."

Pippa clenched her jaw. "That's my mother's best nature talking, not mine," she said, running out of steam.

She no longer had the energy—or the heart—to continue the argument. Not about a will. Not about a non-existent relationship. Not about absolution. Instead she stared out at the city skyline ahead, willing it to come closer faster. A sense of urgency growing in her—or maybe she just wanted to cry in private—Pippa couldn't get back to Westbrook's and away from Sky Thornton soon enough.

When they arrived, Sky drove the four-wheeler through the alleyway, stopping outside the security entrance. On impulse, Pippa dug into her shoulder bag and pulled out what was left of her personal keys, since the car keys had already been stripped from the ring. Hesitating only a moment, she set the ring on the dash.

"My house keys," she explained without looking at Sky. "I have an extra set in my office. You can spend all day searching the house for this supposed new will. Good luck." With that, she hastily pushed open the door.

He grabbed her wrist, forcing her to look at him. "Pippa, please—"

"Just be gone before I get home and leave the keys on the dining-room table."

Ignoring his urgent expression, she tore her arm free and ran, not even bothering to slam the door closed behind her.

And wondered again how she could have been such a fool.

"HOW COULD YOU HAVE BEEN so damn foolish?" Rand demanded, stalking Pippa into her own office before she even had time to remove her coat.

"Good morning to you, too."

"What's so good about finding out my baby sister was attacked and didn't even let me know?"

Hackles raised, emotions stretched beyond endurance after her go-round with Sky, Pippa slammed down her shoulder bag and leaned over her desk. She refused to let another male have the upper hand at the moment. Not even her brother. "First of all, I am not a baby, and it's time you stopped treating me like one."

He waved her objection away. "What did the police do about it?"

"I wouldn't know. I didn't call the police."

Thinking Rand might have an apoplectic fit if his flushed face was any indication, she explained her reasoning, starting with telling him about the caped attacker and ending with what he already knew—

Lieutenant Jackson's firm disbelief in anything she said. Her brother cooled down a bit, though he still wasn't appeased.

"This whole murder thing isn't something to take lightly," he warned her.

"I haven't been." She moved to the window. "I've been doing my best to solve it. With Sky Thornton."

"What!" His shout rose a few decibels. "Pippa, what in the world are you and that...that...moron thinking of?"

Irritated with herself for bristling at his calling Sky a moron, Pippa was even angrier with her brother for questioning her good sense. "I don't know." She glanced at the skaters on the block-square pond below. "Maybe I'm just plain stupid."

Not wanting to stay in his company—or in the store for that matter—she decided this would be the perfect time to run an errand she'd nearly forgotten about. Where were those coalition files?

"Pippa, I didn't mean that."

Spotting the stack of folders on her credenza, she said, "Then start treating me like the adult I am!"

His expression changed before her eyes, going from fury to amusement. "Well, I'll be. You are, aren't you?"

"Surprise, surprise." She flung her leather bag over her shoulder. "Maybe I would have grown up sooner if the McNabb men had allowed me to. No, I take that back. I'm responsible for my own actions," she said, grabbing the files and shoving them into an oversize envelope. "And I'll see you later."

She started to leave but Rand was in the way. "Where are you off to?" he demanded, but when she gave him an aggravated expression, he raised his hands. "In case anyone here needs you."

Still, she couldn't help being defensive. "I have some coalition files to return to Gwen."

"Fine."

"Fine."

With that small victory under her belt, Pippa left the store, walking the several blocks to the coalition offices, forcing her mind—with great difficulty—away from thoughts of Sky.

Arriving via elevator within a few minutes, she was happy to see she was in luck. Gwen was in the reception area talking to the young man seated behind the desk. She appeared a bit drawn, and some of her dark hair had escaped her normally perfect French roll.

Looking up from the messages in her hand, Gwen smiled. "Pippa, how nice to see you."

Pippa forced a smile of her own—no need to let the other woman in on her foul mood—and waved the envelope. "Especially since I'm bearing gifts."

"You found them?"

"Acacia was quite accommodating."

"Really?" Gwen's eyebrows shot up. "Then she must have wanted something."

Odd remark. But with thoughts of Sky on the back burner of her mind, Pippa was easily distracted.

"Let's go into my office," Gwen suggested.

Though she'd only meant to deliver the package and then return to her own office to do some serious thinking—regarding what she was going to do about Sky, about work, about her life—Pippa was grateful for the reprieve. On the way to Gwen's office, they passed a half dozen shabbily dressed people, who sat silent, waiting and expectant, while another worker at a desk talked to one of their number. A counselor, perhaps, trying to get them a meal ticket somewhere. Pippa reminded herself that, compared to them, she had too many blessings to count and that she couldn't let one man bring her down.

Inside the director's office, Gwen slid behind her desk and eagerly ripped open the envelope that Pippa handed her. She immediately sorted through the files, opening a few to check their contents, then leaned back in her chair, her expression thoughtful. "This is it? You're sure Acacia gave them all to you?"

"Actually, she gave us free rein in Lamont's office. We did our own looking."

"We?"

Realizing that if she admitted she was with the man who'd been driving the sleigh that ran over Lamont, the other woman might wonder why they'd been together, Pippa simply said, "A friend." The fewer people who knew about her and Sky's private investigation, the better.

Giving her an arch look, Gwen nodded. "So you gave me everything you found."

"Yes, of course."

But the coalition director seemed dissatisfied, as if she feared Pippa was holding something back from her. What, for heaven's sake?

Before she could question the other woman about specifics, Gwen smiled again, though this time the expression seemed forced. "It's just the tax statement from last year. I hope I can get copies from the IRS, but you know how difficult dealing with the government can be. Well, thanks for your help."

Pippa had the distinct impression she was being dismissed. Not much of a reprieve, after all. "Sorry. If I find the tax statement, I'll be sure to let you know."

With that, she left Gwen's office, distracted by the puzzle of the missing papers. She'd gone all the way down the hall and had pressed the elevator button before she got one of those weird feelings, as if she were being watched. Whipping around, however, she felt foolish. The corridor behind her was empty.

A ding alerted her to the elevator's arrival. Taking a shaky breath, she stepped into the empty car, and with the press of a button, zoomed down to the first floor. There she approached the lobby newsstand concession and gazed at the racks of magazines and newspapers. Anything to stall facing reality.

So why did she have this fantasy that someone was there, scrutinizing her every action? Pippa scanned the crowd around her to no avail. No one seemed in the least bit interested in her activities. Still, she couldn't shake the unsettling feeling.

About to leave, she caught the *Chicago Tribune* headline: Keegan Loses Cool Over Santa Death. Since the story was about the luncheon at Westbrook's, Pippa bought a copy of the newspaper. She was getting her change when she noticed the reflection in the glass. Someone standing a short distance behind her was watching her intently.

She'd recognize that truculent expression anywhere, even if it wasn't topped by a pointed elf hat.

Tightening her hold on her purchase, she spun around just as the dwarf, who was dressed in ragged street clothes, retreated. She went after him, but the little man was too agile for her and somehow did a disappearing act amid the people filing through the building's lobby—stopping Pippa cold.

The dwarf was here, not dressed like an elf, but like a homeless person. And this was the building where the Coalition to Feed the Homeless was housed. Surely no connection was possible. . . .

Gwen's displeasure about the missing documents fresh in her mind, Pippa raced back to the bank of elevators and elbowed her way into a car whose doors were already closing. The doors smacked her, then reopened. She entered and pushed the button for the third floor. Mind spinning, she tried to think of a polite way of putting this situation to the coalition director. But when it came down to it, she chose to be absolutely blunt with Gwen.

Storming into the woman's office without waiting to be announced, she asked, "Are you having one of your homeless people follow me?"

"What?" Perched behind her desk and a mound of paperwork, Gwen gaped. "What in the world are you talking about?"

"A small man," Pippa said, holding her hand below her shoulder to indicate his height. "He sometimes dresses like an elf. I thought he was a Salvation Army volunteer, but maybe he just had a seasonal job for the day. . . ."

Eyes wide, voice controlled, Gwen asked, "What makes you think *I* would want someone to follow you?"

What did? The fact that Gwen seemed dissatisfied with some missing papers simply didn't prove a thing. Suddenly feeling lame, Pippa said, "Well, he looked like he could be one of the homeless people out in your waiting room."

Glaring at her, Gwen hesitated only a second. "I'll call security." Now her voice was tense, making Pippa squirm.

The security person Gwen spoke to promised to have his people on the lookout for the dwarf for questioning.

And feeling foolish, Pippa left again.

Continually craning her head around as she headed back to Westbrook's, Pippa wasn't certain if she was glad or disappointed when she didn't see the man following her, didn't even have a single hair stand on end in warning. She couldn't decide at this point whether she wanted to avoid the whole mystery or resolve it. If only it would just disappear. End.

Like her short-lived relationship with Sky Thornton...the devil who was waiting for her in the executive-floor reception area of Westbrook's.

Sprawled in a leather chair in the seating area, Sky didn't fit into this office environment with his north woods, outdoors image. And yet, to Pippa, he was the best-looking thing in the place. No matter that she couldn't get past his lies, his mere presence made her somehow feel more vital. He'd left an indelible impression on her. Intimate parts of her body were definitely responding to him, despite her newfound will opposing any connection with the man whatsoever. If she couldn't get past this primal attraction when she merely saw him, how would she ever forget their one night together?

Heart pounding at the memory, she softly choked out, "What are you doing here?" past the lump clogging her throat. "I told you to leave the keys. I assume you didn't find the will, because there wasn't anything to find. Right?" When he didn't answer, only continued his steady gaze—his expression open and hungry—she couldn't help taunting him. "Gave up kind of easily, didn't you?"

"I didn't start."

When she realized the receptionist was within earshot, she moved closer to him. "So what are you waiting for? You've wasted half the morning."

"I'm not going to start, Pippa. The will isn't important. It never was. It was a symbol of my brother's forgiveness. You know the concept, don't you?" He stood, his nearness threatening her stability. "And whether or not Dutch wanted to make things up with me isn't important anymore, either."

"Then what is?" She could barely hear the ringing of the phone above the rush of adrenaline coursing through her.

"You."

The receptionist chose that moment to tell her, "Ms. McNabb, you have a call."

A reprieve!

"Thank you, Bridget. I'll take it in my office." She brushed past Sky, who had the audacity to follow on her heels. "Alone," she muttered.

Which he ignored. "We're not finished," he said as they entered her office.

"You're dreaming."

"We have a murder to solve."

Gritting her teeth, Pippa turned her back on him and picked up the receiver. "Pippa McNabb speaking."

"This is Hank, the owner of Broadway Photo Finishers."

Surprised that the owner himself would be calling her, she said, "Did I forget something in the store the other day?"

"Yep. Your photographs."

"You must be mistaken. I took—"

"The wrong packet. Not that it's your fault," he said, rushing to assure her. "Help isn't what it used to be. When Mrs. Anderson came in to get her photos this morning, she wasn't pleased, I can tell you."

Pippa's heart raced. "Are you saying—"

"That my clerk switched packets. I'm terribly sorry about the mix-up."

"So am I. I'll be there as soon as possible to make the switch."

"What switch?" Sky asked from behind her.

After hanging up the receiver, she turned. "The photographs." She was a little stunned by the knowledge. "I was given the wrong photographs!"

"So what are we waiting for?" he asked, taking her arm to guide her out of the room.

Tearing her arm free, she glared at him. "There is no *we*."

"There sure as hell is." He glared back. "Unless you'd like me to inform Lieutenant Isaac Jackson that you're on your way to collect evidence."

Tight-lipped, realizing it would do no good to argue—Sky had his mind made up that she wouldn't get away from him so easily—Pippa raced across the reception area. He'd see she had changed for the better, that she wasn't going to be a pushover for a line some guy she couldn't trust gave her. She hit the call button with more force than she meant to, jarring her still-sore arm.

Through clenched teeth, she asked, "What do you hope to prove by horning in?"

"We're partners, remember?"

The doors swooshed open.

"I remember a lot of things."

"Some of which I hope to convince you to forget."

"Don't count on it," she muttered as she entered the empty car and pressed the first-floor button.

Only after the doors had closed and the elevator had started its descent did he admit, "I've never been able to count on anything or anyone for as long as I can remember."

That got to her for a moment. She'd always had a family to back her up, while his had deserted him. Not just his brother, but his mother, as well. No wonder trust didn't come easily to him. Still . . .

"That was no reason to seduce me under false pretenses!"

"Seduce? That was no seduction," he stated as the car bounced to a stop and the doors whooshed open. "You were as hot for me as I was for you last night!"

Pippa felt her face flame as she pushed her way through a crowd of people who were too interested in their argument for her comfort. She headed for an exit.

"Wait a minute." Sky was directly behind her. "Where are you going?"

"To hail a taxi. I don't have a car, remember."

"Taxi? Bull!" Sky cuffed her wrist and pulled her toward an alley exit.

"Take your hands off me, or I'll call for security."

"I am your security, if only you would realize it."

"You're my worst nightmare come true."

His jaw clenched, his body tensed, but he didn't let go.

And Pippa didn't call for anyone.

SKY WAS CONTENT TO LET Pippa have her peace for the moment. She deserved it, deserved so much more than he'd given her. Mainly his trust. Only trust was a difficult thing for him to come by. No excuses. He should have told her. He'd had days to change his mind about her, days to reveal his true identity. He had no one to blame but himself. Therefore, he should leave her alone. But he couldn't. Not until he was certain she would be safe. If nothing else, he could give her the gift of his protection.

They didn't speak to each other again until after they'd arrived at Broadway Photo Finishers and Pippa had made the switch. Then, a few minutes later, sitting in the Ranger, hands shaking, she opened the packet, saying, "Pray this set of photos is more enlightening than the last."

She pulled out the first photograph and Sky moved closer to look. The fact that she stiffened didn't get by him. He refused to move, inhaling her scent as he nearly wound himself over her shoulder to see a picture of a construction site. As she shuffled through the rest, he noticed all of them were similar—different views of the same project.

She moaned, "Oh, no. All those expectations for nothing."

"What did you think? That the killer would take self-portraits?" Then Sky flashed in a hand and plucked the photos from her. "Wait a minute. Look at this one." He was staring at a horizontal shot, with the city skyline in the background.

"What am I looking at?"

"Isn't this a bit familiar?"

On the verge of denying it, she stopped and grew thoughtful. "The newspaper clipping. Mayor Keegan with a shovel. The ground breaking of the City Streets development. There has to be a connection, but what?"

"Look at these," he said, indicating three more shots. "This clearly shows the billboard declaring the site is being developed by Metropolis Construction."

"So?"

"Who owns Metropolis Construction?"

Pippa shrugged. "I don't have the faintest idea."

"The city or state would," Sky mused.

"And can you imagine how much red tape would be involved in finding out through government channels. Besides, this is the Thursday before a holiday weekend," she reminded him. "Since Christmas Eve and Day fall on Saturday and Sunday, government offices are already closed."

"Damn!"

"But why is this so important?" she asked.

"It may not be...unless Mayor Darby Keegan has some kind of vested interest in the company that's building on what used to be Chicago Housing Authority land. We have to figure some way of finding out more about Metropolis Construction."

"Frank Hatcher."

"The data processing nerd?"

"Manager," she corrected, a hint of excitement creeping into her tone. "He probably has access to any sources we might need."

"You think he'll do it?"

"He wouldn't dare say no."

Chapter Thirteen

Despite that confident statement, Frank Hatcher did try to say no. Then Pippa got tough, surprising the hell out of Sky. She threatened to bring up his nefarious activities for Lamont at the next board meeting.

Before his amazed eyes, his innocent angel blackmailed the poor bastard into doing what she wanted!

Desperation often made a person do or say things they never would otherwise, Sky thought. He was a prime example. If only he could explain... "I loved my brother once upon a time," he said, intending to make the attempt.

"So did I." Her soft voice hardened. "Until I learned who the real Bertram 'Dutch' Vanleer was."

After hours, they were waiting in her office for whatever information Hatcher could track. And Sky figured that gave him time enough to make his case. She sat behind her desk looking depressed and tired as hell. Feeling old beyond his years himself, he paced the length of the room.

"Dutch wasn't always the rotten bastard he ended up being. I mean, he was always full of himself, but he also cared about other people. Me, at least."

"You were close?"

Remembering how close, Sky nodded. "I had a hard time with Nola divorcing my father. I had a hard time with having to call her Nola." A kid should be able to be a kid. Sometimes he felt as if both their childhoods had been stolen. "Dutch wasn't happy with the situation, either, though he hid it better than I did. He and I... well, we stuck together. No matter what, we had each other. He was my big brother, and he took care of me."

Until Vanessa.

"I thought he would take care of me, too," she admitted. "And it's what I thought I wanted at the time."

Sky would love the opportunity to take care of Pippa, though he dared not say so, not with the way things stood between them. "It's only natural... needing another person." He needed her more than anyone he'd ever known.

"I was right out of school, confused about my role as a modern woman," she was saying. "On the one hand, I was supposed to have a career, find some way to use the education I'd worked so hard to get. On the other hand, I wanted to be like my mother and raise a family."

"Nothing wrong with that. Sounds pretty good to me."

"It was great. Mom was always there for us kids because she stayed at home rather than get a job. We didn't have much—five kids on a cop's pay—but we didn't care. We felt like we had everything important in life."

If only he and Dutch could have had a mother like hers, things might have turned out differently for both of them. "You were lucky."

"Blessed."

Their gazes connected . . . as for a moment did their hearts.

"I got it!" Without preamble, Frank Hatcher entered her office, smashing the auspicious and precious moment into smithereens. He was waving several slips of paper at them.

"What did you find?" Pippa asked anxiously, popping up out of her chair.

"Metropolis Construction was owned by two other companies—All-City Contractors and Best-Way Builders."

That couldn't be all. The nervous little man almost looked ready to burst as Pippa rounded the desk.

Obligingly, Sky prompted him. "And . . ."

"Best-Way is owned by a guy named Louis D'Angelo. All-City has three partners—Gary Michaels, Terrance Kloss and Elaine Donovan."

"And?" Pippa echoed Sky, her expression a mix of disappointment and trust that there was more.

"On further investigation, I learned Elaine Donovan's maiden name was—"

"Keegan!" Sky and Pippa both said at once.

"You got it." With a grimace, Hatcher handed her the computer printouts and checked his watch. "Can I go home now?"

"Go already," Pippa said, her expression relieved.

Hatcher made for the door, stopping only to say, "I assume we're square?"

"You and I are, yes," she assured him. "I can't promise to lie for you, but I won't volunteer information about anything you've done under duress, either . . . uh, as long as you don't volunteer anything about what we told you or asked you to do tonight."

Making a noise of disgust, Hatcher fled the office.

Realizing she'd done it again, had used subtle black-mail to keep the data processing manager quiet about their activities, Sky wasn't certain whether he should be proud of Pippa ... or disappointed in her.

"So, do we assume Elaine Donovan is the mayor's daughter?" he asked.

"A daughter or a sister. Either way, we've got him."

"For what?"

"For Lamont's murder."

Hating to burst her balloon, he said, "You're rushing things. Lamont might have known about the mayor's financial interests, but that's not proof of anything to do with his murder."

"But if Keegan was the one who dropped the roll of film—"

"He wasn't. Keegan wouldn't have taken those pictures," Sky said with certainty. "Why would he have connected himself to the construction site after burying his financial interest in it? No, I think our photographer was someone who wanted to implicate His Honor, the Mayor, in his under-the-table dealings—someone who wanted him to end up in the mud exactly as Lamont did."

"And then Keegan found out about it and killed Lamont to shut him up."

"Maybe."

"So who would know about the underhanded deal?" Pippa mused, continuing in the same vein. "Other than some member of his staff."

As she passed him, her subtle scent distracted him for a moment. Then, telling himself this wasn't the time for distractions, Sky said, "Valerie did a disappearing act the day of the luncheon."

"So?"

"Let's say she somehow knew you found the roll of film and had it developed. What if she was searching your office for the photographs, and when she didn't find them, decided to wait for you outside."

"Wearing the cape she stole from me."

"Exactly. I think it's time I got together with Valerie Quinlan for some straight talk," he proposed.

"Good. Let's get going."

"Not us. Me. I'll have a better chance with her alone."

Pippa set her jaw. "I'll bet."

"Jealous?" Sky raised his brows. "I'll take that as a compliment."

And an indication that Pippa was still interested in a relationship with him, if only he could find a way to redeem himself in her eyes. Maybe bringing a murderer to justice was a step in the right direction.

PIPPA WAITED to change directions until she was certain Sky was far enough away that he couldn't stop her.

"I'm not going home, after all," Pippa told the taxi driver. "Head for Winnetka…and be prepared to wait for me for a return to the city."

"Yes, ma'am!"

Fat chance she'd sit around twiddling her thumbs at home, pining away for Sky's promised call while he was busy with the lovely blond Valerie. Realizing that he'd been correct—that she *was* jealous—Pippa shifted uncomfortably in the back seat. She'd thought she was done with the man, and while saddened by the death of what had seemed to be a promising relationship, part of her had also been relieved.

Hadn't she decided that she didn't need a relationship with any man until she figured out what she wanted to do with her life?

Choosing to put her personal problems on hold at least for the present, she tore her mind away from the vivid sensual images of Sky that continued to taunt her and reassigned her attention to the investigation.

It hadn't taken her but a moment to decide on another visit with Acacia Birch. Surely, if Lamont had information about Keegan's financial interests, he would have told his wife. With a little serious prompting, maybe Acacia could shed additional light on their investigation.

She only hoped the long taxi ride wouldn't be for nothing. What if Acacia wasn't home...

Nearly forty minutes later, a servant was showing her inside the lakefront mansion and relieving that particular anxiety. "If you would wait in the parlor, I'll tell Mrs. Birch that you're here."

Pippa had barely removed her coat and settled herself on a sofa in front of the crackling fire before she heard the click of high heels on the marble entryway. She turned to greet the lady of the manor. "Hello, Acacia."

"Pippa, dear, what a surprise. Again."

Today the widow was wearing black...in the form of a revealing, lace-trimmed negligee and peignoir that swirled around her as she swept into the room. Pippa wondered if she'd interrupted something. Again.

And something Gwen said days ago came back to her—that Acacia had threatened to see Lamont dead before giving him a divorce. Had he been threatening her because of *her* affair rather than one of his own?

"Have you come to return that file on Darby Keegan?" Acacia asked, her tone hopeful.

Giving Pippa the perfect lead-in. "Not exactly. But Mayor Keegan *is* my reason for being here. Sky and I took a good, hard look at those clippings, then did some research." True to her word to Hatcher, she didn't say how. "Have you ever heard of Elaine Donovan?"

"Keegan's sister?"

That confirmed it. "Exactly," an elated Pippa said as if she'd been certain all along. "Well, it seems the mayor was the chief influence in having several buildings of a housing project razed . . . only to have an elaborate complex built on what had been prime Chicago Housing Authority land. We did some digging into the construction company and traced a connection to Elaine."

An odd expression crossed Acacia's classical features—triumph mixed with relief?—that gave Pippa pause.

"Then Lamont was correct," his widow said.

"So you knew all about it?"

"Certainly not the details, but Lamont did pose the theory as a means of getting the dirt on Keegan." She smoothed the silver streak in her hair. "I thought he was fabricating it because he was so set on this ridiculous election idea."

Acacia's obvious contempt for public service irritated Pippa. "I don't think wanting to be mayor of Chicago was a ridiculous dream." Though she'd have had serious reservations about Lamont being any better at the job than Keegan, considering his methods. Blackmail was a criminal offense.

"It is ridiculous if you don't have the money to finance your campaign," Acacia was saying.

"I had the impression that Lamont had some independent wealth."

"*Had* being the operative word. He lived quite nicely off my money, yes, after he squandered his own." Acacia sighed and shook her head sadly. "I'm afraid dear Lamont had a bit of a gambling problem."

A problem that was news to Pippa. Frowning, she asked, "And you weren't interested in backing him?"

"No. And since one needs a good deal of money to run a campaign of that magnitude, and since Lamont had only involved himself in politics in peripheral ways, it wasn't likely he'd have gotten the support of his party, either."

"Even running as an independent, he could have raised the necessary funds."

"Given enough time and a loyal cadre of workers, yes. But the next election was too close to raise the money or the support he needed. I'm afraid his bid for mayor was nothing but a pipe dream. A dead end."

As was Pippa's visit.

On the way back to the city, however, she couldn't help thinking that Acacia had had a hidden agenda in revealing as much as she had. She couldn't forget about that moment when the widow had revealed her true emotions—triumph and relief.

About what?

Pippa also figured that Lamont must have had some ace up his sleeve where the needed money was concerned. He wasn't a stupid man. And as far as she knew, he was crafty rather than delusional. So, Acacia wouldn't give Lamont the money to run a mayoral campaign. He must have had a backup plan to get it or he wouldn't have challenged Keegan at the fund-raiser.

Backup plan... backup apartment... Lamont's city residence.

That was it—her next move.

"I don't want to go home, after all," she told the taxi driver.

"Big surprise," he muttered good-naturedly.

She had no doubt she could find Lamont's city address in the store's personnel records. The last time she and Sky had visited her, Acacia had said her late husband had used that address on his income-tax returns.

"Take me back to Westbrook's, instead."

As for getting into Lamont's city hideaway... since she always kept a backup set of personal keys at the office, Pippa was gambling that Lamont did, too.

SKY TOOK A BIG GAMBLE when he finally tracked Valerie down at a bar frequented by politicians. Easily getting her away from her cohorts into a quiet, dark booth in the corner, he began by asking her, "Where did you go when you disappeared from Mayor Keegan's luncheon yesterday?"

The tightening of her hands around her mug of beer was barely perceptible. "I didn't go anywhere."

He took a sip from his mug. He'd chosen to take his coffee straight to keep his faculties clear. "I was there, Valerie," he finally said. "You weren't in the room."

"I wasn't hungry. So I went outside to get away from Mayor Keegan's tiresome maneuvering. I thought maybe some Christmas music and a few minutes counting the ornaments on Westbrook's atrium tree would relieve some of the tension I've been under lately."

"You're lying."

"How dare you!" she said hotly, though she kept her voice low, then took a quick look around as if to make certain she'd drawn no attention to herself.

"Because I was outside the room with Pippa. And you weren't."

"I did get some fresh air—"

"Stop lying, Valerie. We have the photographs."

"Photographs?"

The mayor's aide was trying to bluff him, but he didn't miss the change in her tone. He was certain she knew exactly what photographs he meant. He had her. He could practically smell her fear.

"The ones Pippa had developed of the City Streets Complex construction site and the Metropolis Construction signs," he said, watching her expression carefully. She didn't bluff well. "The ones you tried to steal from Pippa's office that afternoon while we were busy with the mayor. And the very same ones you attacked her to get."

"What?" Valerie sounded panicked. And the panic sounded real, her voice rising several decibels. "I never attacked anyone!"

Sky halfway believed her. "So you didn't don a green cape, carry a brick and wait for Pippa to leave last evening?"

"No! Oh, my God..." She gasped, tried to get a grip on herself. Instead her eyes filled with tears. "I should have stopped before it got this far. Only I couldn't. He blackmailed me into going through with it. Don't you see? I had no choice. Yes, I searched Pippa's office for the photographs, but I didn't try to hurt her. I would never hurt anyone." A beat later, she asked, "Is Pippa all right?"

"As well as can be expected," Sky said, figuring Valerie's "he" referred to Lamont Birch. Was there no end to the bastard's blackmail victims? "Pippa got away with a few bruises." When Valerie sighed with relief, Sky struck again. "What about you? Did you kill Lamont?"

Her eyes widened and a tear streaked down her cheek. "God, no!"

"Then who did?"

"Like I told Lieutenant Jackson I—I don't know."

But it sounded like she had her suspicions—no doubt His Honor, the Mayor. Not wanting to voice that assumption, he said, "So why don't you start at the beginning."

Shuddering, she took in a long draft of beer. "I shouldn't say anything. I should get a lawyer."

"Why do you need a lawyer if you haven't committed a crime? Besides, I'm not the police. Remember, I'm the person who was inadvertently responsible for the man's death because of someone else."

"That is horrible," she admitted, slumping back into her corner of the booth. "All right. I'll tell you what I know."

"Good."

After fortifying herself with another slug of beer, she began, "I got into politics because I wanted to do something meaningful with my life. I thought Mayor Keegan was an honest, if somewhat controversial, man. I learned otherwise. If I had gone to the press directly, the scandal would have ruined me. No one in government would have given me a job if my name was even mentioned. Politicians like to think the people who work for them are loyal, no matter what."

"So you went to Lamont."

She nodded. "I knew he hated Keegan. I figured he'd be able to use the information. He ended up using it against me, plus some information that I'd once been arrested—"

"For what?" Sky interrupted.

"Political activism in college. I only spent a couple of days in jail, but that was enough for me. And for him to hold over my head. Plus, he said if I didn't continue to provide him with information, he would reveal his source. I, uh, tried to limit the damage by starting a more personal relationship with Lamont."

"You became his mistress?"

She flushed. "It was stupid. Unnecessary. It didn't let me off the hook. And then, to top it off, his wife came to see me about what she called our 'sordid little affair.'"

"Acacia?" Funny that the black widow had never mentioned Valerie.

"She told me not to get out of line and overestimate Lamont's affections for me. She said she would rather see him dead than divorced from her. Maybe she carried through with her threat."

So Valerie suspected Acacia Birch rather than the mayor. Interesting. And something he definitely intended to share with Pippa the moment he could get to a telephone.

But after paying the check and taking his leave of Valerie, Sky was livid when he did make that call from a pay phone. Pippa allowed her machine to answer. Slamming down the receiver in the middle of her message, he vowed to tell her exactly what he thought of her attempts to avoid him when he arrived on her doorstep and faced her down.

SINCE THEY SEEMED to be sharing everything, they would come face-to-face with the truth if only they took their blinders off.

Sky Thornton, half brother to Dutch Vanleer, late husband of Pippa McNabb. Yes, she knew who he was. Lamont had taught her well.

She knew everything there was to know about them. She'd made it her business, even as she'd hoped they would give up and leave the investigation to the police. Bad enough to have the authorities involved. They would get to the truth eventually, even though she'd misdirected them as much as possible.

Only two days to go. Two days to carry out the plan that Lamont had forced her to put into action. Unfortunately, it wouldn't be two days without further interference.

Regretfully, she was going to have to take care of Sky and Pippa the way she had Lamont. . . .

OBTAINING INFORMATION about Lamont Birch's city address was even easier than Pippa had anticipated.

Upon arriving at the executive floor of Westbrook's, she unlocked the receptionist's desk for the master key that would let her into the lawyer's office. In doing so, she found Bridget's book of home addresses and telephone numbers of the executive staff. Hurriedly she scribbled down information about the nearby Plymouth Court residence and stuffed it into her shoulder bag. Then, leaving the purse and her coat at the receptionist's desk, Pippa went after the spare set of apartment keys she was hoping the lawyer had kept in his office.

As she searched, she ruminated on Sky's perfidy and all his talk of a second will. Why would he believe Nola, after what she'd done to him? Pippa guessed he was desperate for some sense of family. Maybe she ought to be more understanding and forgive him. Realizing she was letting Sky Thornton get to her without his even being present, Pippa concentrated on her search.

But after going through every desk and file drawer in the office, she had nothing to show for her trouble. It seemed she wasn't destined to find anything, after all. She looked around the room for another possible hiding place, and her gaze locked on the small safe buried within the bookshelves. Could it be...?

Problem was, she didn't have the combination. But Rand did.

She wasted no time in getting to the desk phone and punching out her brother's home number. Two rings and Rand himself answered. But, rather than giving her the information she rapidly requested, he demanded, "What are you doing at the store at this time of night?"

"Oh, come on," she said, trying not to sound impatient. "It's only a little after ten."

"Closer to eleven."

"Don't split hairs. Do you have the combination or not?"

"What's going on?" Shelby asked from some distance.

Pippa also caught Rand's muffled response. "My little sister is trying to prove how grown-up she is." He'd obviously covered the receiver with his hand so she wouldn't hear.

She told herself to count to ten and be pleasant.

"So why do you need to get into Lamont's safe?"

"Some tax info for the coalition is still missing, and I thought it might be in there," Pippa fibbed, saying the first thing that came to mind...though it *could be* true.

Obviously it was enough to appease him. Rand said, "There's a leather-bound ledger in my office, locked in the file drawer of my desk. The key for that should be on Bridget's ring along with the master."

"Right," she said, after checking it. "I see several desk keys."

"When you find the ledger, you'll find various safe combinations on a middle page. Lamont's is coded L.E.G."

"Got it. Thanks."

"And Pippa...you don't need to prove anything to me, okay? After you check the safe, go straight home."

"I'll leave right afterward," she hedged, hating to lie outright. She would leave...but for Lamont's apartment. "Give my love to Shelby."

Less than ten minutes later, she'd found the combination and was using it on the safe.

Right past zero twice, stop on three. Left past zero twice, stop on six. Right past zero once, stop on four. Right past zero once, stop on seven. Click.

"That's it!" she cried triumphantly, wrenching the handle. The door swung open smoothly. Pippa reached in, moved aside some papers, and at the back of the safe, her fingers hit jingling metal. "Eureka!"

Keys in hand, Pippa made a cursory inspection of the safe's other contents, but nothing jumped out at her as being of any importance to the investigation. Of course, she *was* tired. If she didn't find anything of value at Lamont's apartment, she could come back to the safe and give the contents a closer check.

She backtracked through the offices, shutting off lights, getting her coat, stuffing the keys into her shoulder bag. Then she dialed the in-store number for Edgar Siefert, the night security guard, to tell him she was on her way down. No answer. She let it ring nearly a dozen times. Edgar must be on his rounds of the store.

Shrugging, Pippa made for the elevator, but hitting the call button didn't open the doors. She'd been so busy she hadn't heard the car descend. She glanced up at the row of numbers indicating the floors . . . the five was lit up.

The security guard was probably checking out the fifth floor and had pulled the stop button while he did so. He seemed to have forgotten about her. Oh well, she could always use the emergency stairs.

A flicker of unease twitched through her, but she told herself she was being foolish. Pippa stalled, undecided for a moment. The stairs would probably be faster than waiting for the elevator to be back in service. And she was in Westbrook's, her own store, for heaven's sake. What did she have to be nervous about?

Chastising herself, she entered the stairwell. If there were ever a fire, floodlights on each level would go on, but now they were dark. A single, caged bulb next to each door provided her with the only illumination.

She started down, her rubber-soled boots shooshing over the concrete stairs, the spooky sound raising the flesh along her arms. She passed the eighth floor . . . seventh . . . sixth . . . fifth. Halfway there.

About to pass the fourth, she heard a noise above her . . . like a door opening. "Edgar?" she called out, her voice echoing through the concrete and metal stairwell. She paused on the landing. "Is that you?"

No answer.

A chill shot through Pippa, and yet she resolutely refused to be spooked. Old buildings made creepy noises. And Westbrook's was nearly a century old. The building was settling. That had to be it.

But as she descended, she listened hard, and swore she caught the click of a hard leather heel on a concrete step. No fool, she moved faster, practically flying down the remaining dimly lit stairs. Past three. Another sound above. Two. She glanced upward. A mistake. Her right heel slipped on the edge of a stair. Her ankle wrenched. Swallowing a cry, Pippa was lucky to catch hold of the rail. Stopped momentarily, she caught her breath.

Was someone on the stairs above her or not? Her heart pounded as she searched the shadows. If so, that someone was up to no good.

The murderer?

Her mouth went dry. Sudden, absolute fear gnawing at her, Pippa edged down the final flight to the ground floor. She hung on to the railing for support while repeatedly glancing up over her shoulder.

Did that shadow move?

Pippa prayed her imagination was hard at work, but by the time she got to the first-floor landing, she was panicked and shaking and covered in a light sweat. She threw the door open only to be blasted by a Christmas carol.

"Deck the halls with boughs of holly..."

Blocking her ears against the raucous music, she limped across the floor in the near dark, her eyes adjusting to the faint glow coming from the street through the store's windows. And she could see a sliver of light ahead—the security guard's station. Anything but jolly, as the irritating song claimed she should be, Pippa headed directly for that office. Sounds seemed to be coming from everywhere now.

"Edgar!" she called over the blasting music, remembering he had a gun. "Edgar, where the hell are you!"

Suddenly a silhouette slipped out from the shadows directly between her and the security station.

"Thank God," she said, stopping, relief making her go limp.

"Don we now our gay apparel..."

And then she realized the silhouette was wearing a cape with a hood.

The murderer was indeed stalking her!

Chapter Fourteen

Pippa immediately shifted gears, rushing at the nearby door to the alley. A woman's soft laughter from behind raised her hackles. The door was locked. She slapped at the glass, which vibrated dangerously under her hand. *Don't panic!* The keys were in her shoulder bag. In plunged her hand...only to meet three sets. Store. Home. And Lamont's.

And the caped figure was drawing closer.

Pippa removed her hand with the keys. *House keys! Damn!* She dropped them back into the bag, fingers too clumsy to try again, her mind spinning with possibilities. Certain that a woman was lurking in the velvet's folds, Pippa thought about challenging her. But then she remembered how strong the murderer had been when fighting for her shoulder bag. And she might be armed.

That thought quickly translated into flight. Ignoring the pain shooting through the ankle she'd twisted, she flew toward the escalator.

"Follow me in merry measure..." instructed the recorded Christmas carol.

The caped murderer was indeed following, and from the ruckus beyond, back in the security area, Edgar must have finally come to his senses. He was armed, she reminded herself. That meant she just had to stay safe until he could get to her.

"Edgar, this way! Lower level!" she shouted.

No answer.

Holding on to both sides of the stopped escalator, Pippa, careful of her ankle, jounced down the metal stairs to the lower level. Only red exit lights broke the dark. Her stomach was knotted, her breathing labored. But the moment she was off the escalator, she called on her native ingenuity to find some makeshift form of protection.

"You won't get away, Pippa," came a muffled woman's voice over the final, *Fa la la la la* of "Deck the Halls."

Pippa would have liked to do some decking herself, but she was in no position to chance confronting the murderer up close and personal. Instead, by instinct and a good memory, she traced her way through the dark to the small-appliance department—her last assignment before catering—and armed herself.

"It's no use, Pippa," came that same muffled, rasping voice. "I can't let you leave alive."

"And I can't let you kill me!" Pippa shouted, wondering what the heck was taking Edgar so long to come to her rescue.

"You're weak. Pathetic. You can't stop me."

Pippa listened intently to the voice, then yelled, "I can try!" and flung an iron with all her might in that direction. A *thunk* and a cry told her she'd hit her mark.

Next she found a large meat cleaver, but try as she might, she couldn't force herself to use it. She *was* weak. She couldn't chance killing a killer. Hurting that killer to stop her, however, was another story.

The woman's voice rasping, "Now you've made me angry," made Pippa panicky.

Feeling along another counter, she grasped a slender handle. "Come closer and I'll ruin your face," she warned the other woman, snapping on the switch to the battery-operated mixer. Nothing happened. Kids must have been fooling with it again—the display unit was out of power. "Damn!"

Manic laughter sent chills scurrying up Pippa's spine... and sent Pippa scurrying through the underground level and tossing a waffle iron at the murderer to slow her down.

Where the hell was the security guard? It didn't look like Edgar was going to show. Fearing she was on her own, after all, Pippa thought fast. She had to get out of the store. While sprinting for the exit doors leading directly into the pedway—the subterranean footpath that lay directly beneath the entire Loop area—she searched her bag for the store keys. At first, she couldn't sort them out. Then, fingers running over the small desk keys, she snatched the store ring in triumph. She headed for the red exit sign and practically crashed into the door.

"There you are," came the relentless voice, drawing ever closer.

Pippa fumbled but finally found the right key, unlocked the door and stumbled into the pedway. Her leather-soled boots squished creepily against the day's muck that had been dragged down there. The place was eerie. During the day, the pedway seemed so safe, filled with people hustling and bustling from building to building. At this time of night, it was dank—stifling. But a safe haven for the homeless against the night's bitter cold and threat of more snow.

Leaving her keys in the door lest they delay her long enough to be caught, Pippa flew down the passageway. Ahead, a sleeping man covered with cardboard lay on his side. A woman with arms protectively surrounding her two small children huddled opposite. Startled by Pippa's unexpected approach, the mother hugged her kids closer as Pippa ran past.

At an intersection, Pippa quickly glanced over her shoulder at the caped woman and the blur of movement farther back. She chose the left branch that eventually led to the rapid transit entrance—and hopefully other people, maybe even police—and forced herself to run faster until her ankle burned as if it was on fire.

Athletes could do it. They could run on injuries. She could do anything if she tried hard enough, Pippa told herself for maybe the millionth time.

As she ran, she speculated on the murderer's identity. Acacia Birch sprang to mind immediately, undoubtedly because she'd just confronted the widow.

"Pippa!" The familiar male voice cut through further deliberation.

"Sky?" Slowing, she glanced over her shoulder again.

The caped woman turned, too, and then in a sudden burst of speed, caught up to Pippa, rammed her off balance and set off down the tunnel toward the rapid transit line.

"Don't let her get away!" Pippa yelled at Sky, already limping in the new direction herself.

"Are you all right?"

"The murderer!" she gasped, shoving him after the woman, who was now approaching the other end of the tunnel and the turnstiles.

Now that the urgency to save her skin was lessened, Pippa realized she was out of steam. She stumbled to a slow jog, watching Sky's broad frame shoot away from her.

When he got to the entrance, he jumped the turnstile and ran down the stairs, angering the lone employee in a booth, who called, "Transit Police!" over the loudspeaker. "Gate jumper. He's wearing a—"

"Don't!" Pippa yelled over the rumble of a train below, rushing ahead once more. "I'll pay for him."

Breathlessly she retrieved her wallet and found two tokens, which she pushed at the CTA employee. Then she bulldozed her way through the turnstile to the stairs. A few steps down she had a perfect view of train doors whooshing shut in Sky's face. Or rather, the outstretched arm that snapped back fast out of harm's way. Realizing it was no use, she stopped. The train shot off, leaving Pippa with the impression of a green blur at a window.

Ignoring the Up escalator, Sky took two stairs at a time to join her. "Sorry," he said, taking a big breath.

"I'm not." Truth welling in her, Pippa started back to the landing. "I was never so glad to see anyone in my life." And not just because he'd saved her skin.

"That's encouraging."

To counter the thrill that shot through her at the low cadence of his voice, she added, "Though I'd been hoping for the security guard."

Taking her arm, Sky muttered some response she probably wasn't meant to understand, moved her out into the passageway and turned in the direction from which they'd come. Halfway back to the store, he told her, "I broke into Westbrook's through the security station. I could see the guard through the window. He was out cold."

Pippa's heart jumped to her throat. "Oh, Lord, no wonder Edgar didn't answer." What if he wasn't just unconscious? "We'd better get back there, quick.

He didn't argue, but took off at a brisk pace that made her ankle beg for mercy. He didn't seem to notice that she was limping slightly. "The security guard will be all right," he said reassuringly as they sped along. "I called 9-1-1 and made sure he was conscious. That's what took me so long to come after you. When I heard you scream . . ."

His grim tone thrilled her. He obviously cared what happened to her. Not that she should be thrilled. Pippa warned herself not to let her guard down.

But as they passed the homeless people who'd been there earlier, Pippa started digging in her bag for some money. Sky beat her to it. He slipped the mother a twenty and the guy who was now awake a ten. If she wasn't careful, she would fall in love with him all over again.

This time securing the door and taking her keys after they reentered the store, Pippa groused to herself, "*Love!*" Nothing good had ever come of it, not the man-woman kind, not for her.

"Did you say something?"

"No."

Suddenly grinning, he wouldn't let it alone. "I could have sworn you did."

"Better get your hearing checked." Then, looking around at the lower level, she realized she could see clearly. "The lights are on."

"And from the sound of it, the police have arrived." Indeed, the muffled thuds overhead were unmistakably footsteps.

"Let's go face the music." Which, at the moment, happened to be "Have Yourself a Merry Little Christmas." "Bah, humbug!" Pippa grumbled as she hobbled toward the elevator.

TO SKY'S AMAZEMENT, Pippa was still grumbling when, after checking out the store and taking down a report, the police left. Over Edgar's protestations that he was fine, just had a little lump on his noggin, she'd sent him to the emergency room to be checked out. His replacement had arrived and was on the job.

Free to leave, she muttered, "When is this crimson nightmare going to end?"

Sky had never seen her in such a negative mood. Though he supposed being stalked by a killer was bound to turn the best of attitudes bad, he hoped he had something to do with her grumpiness—or rather, her realization that she had feelings for him despite what he'd done. His hopes that she could find forgiveness in her heart grew a tad brighter.

The young security guard was locking the alleyway door behind them when Sky said, "I'll take you home."

"I'm not going home."

"Hospital?"

"No. I'll call to check on Edgar later."

"You have a midnight rendezvous planned?" Sky persisted.

"Something like that."

Steering her to the Ranger, Sky told himself not to react. No need to be jealous. He'd bet anything Pippa didn't have a late date—she wasn't the kind of woman who held one man on a string while sleeping with another. He unlocked the door and helped her in. But she was up to something.

He waited until he'd started the vehicle before asking, "So where are we going? And before you object, you better just resign yourself to my being your shadow until the murderer is caught. I'm not taking any more chances with your life."

"As if you were responsible." Sighing deeply, she gave up without a fight. "Plymouth Court. Lamont's city apartment. I have the keys."

Though he thought of suggesting the keys might open Birch's Winnetka residence, he didn't. Good thing, because he would have been wrong.

The apartment actually turned out to be a loft, with an office on the wall-free second floor, which overlooked the living and sleeping arrangements on the open lower level.

"What are we trying to find?" Sky asked as he began searching the desk while she attacked the file drawers.

"I didn't get that far," she admitted. "Anything that seems relevant."

"To whom?"

"The suspects."

"Acacia Birch," he said.

"Gwen Walsh."

"Why her?"

"There was this dwarf who followed me...never mind. Let's just say Gwen's in the running." She pulled out a folder, gave it a quick once-over, then shoved it back in place. "And Valerie Quinlan, right?"

Thinking about his conversation with the mayor's aide, Sky couldn't argue. "So you think your attacker tonight was a woman."

Pippa nodded. "I'm certain that was no man threatening to kill me."

"But you didn't recognize the voice?"

"It was muffled, like she was speaking through cloth."

"Maybe she had a scarf around her mouth."

They let the subject drop and continued the search with a vengeance. He'd certainly like to wreak some vengeance on the woman who'd tried to kill Pippa. If only he'd moved a bit faster. He'd actually had the velvet cloak in his grasp a second before the doors had snapped shut, threatening to take his hand along with the moving train.

While the side desk drawers yielded nothing of interest—mostly paperwork on Birch's own financial affairs—the center drawer refused to open. "Do you have a key to this desk?" Sky asked.

"Nope. Only the downstairs and apartment keys."

"Let's see if I can jimmy it open." He picked up a letter opener.

"Another one of those survival skills?"

Annoyed at the intimation—as if, because he hadn't told her who he was, he was dishonest at heart—Sky said, "Watch, and maybe you'll learn something."

But Pippa was too busy, glued to one of the hanging file folders she'd dug out of the drawer she was working on. "I think I found it," she said, even as the desk-drawer lock gave with a *clunk*.

"What?" The center drawer held little more than a bankbook with several recent, healthy-size deposits, certainly larger than Birch's payroll checks would be.

Pippa distracted him from the bankbook by setting the folder down on the desktop and spreading out the newspaper clippings she removed. "Looks like this could be another blackmail victim."

The clippings were nearly two decades old, the stories detailing the arrest and conviction of a mother-daughter scam operation. Winona Sarcosi had been in her late teens, her mother June, in her mid-thirties. They'd presented the girl as the illegitimate daughter of a prominent businessman, and then had blackmailed him for their silence. The injured wife had found out, anyway, and the scandal had hit the press, though it was learned afterward that other wealthy men had been presented with the very same "illegitimate" daughter. The two had been living off the scam for years.

"Lamont was the victim's personal lawyer," Pippa said. "He pressed the prosecution to go for the maximum penalty."

"It's ironic, isn't it, Birch going after someone else for blackmail—his specialty—but why do you think it's relevant?"

"The daughter got out." Pippa showed him another newspaper article dated several years later. Standing so close he was hard-pressed to pay attention. "But the mother died in a prison ruckus just one week before her release date. Had she not gotten the maximum sentence..."

"She would still be alive."

"That gives the daughter a pretty strong motive. Winona could be any one of them—Acacia, Gwen, Valerie."

"Winona has dark hair," Sky said, indicating one of the photos. "Valerie's a blonde."

Pippa snorted. "Don't be naive."

The look she gave him was one of affectionate disbelief. Okay, so maybe Valerie had changed the color of her hair. And she had already admitted to being blackmailed by Birch for having spent a few days in jail....

Jail!

"What about Connie?" he suggested. "She's served time."

"For accessory to auto theft. Besides, her name is really Connie Ortega. Frank Hatcher did a thorough search of her past, remember. If it was an alias, he would have known."

"And Acacia Birch is too high profile to be operating under an assumed identity."

"That leaves Gwen and Valerie," Pippa said.

"Too bad no one got a better shot of the daughter's face."

The photo used to accompany most of the articles was of mother and daughter, Winona's face pressed into June's breast. In others, Winona Sarcosi's head was bent and her long, dark hair covered most of her face.

Figuring they had what they came for, they bundled up the file into a large envelope and started to leave. Only then did Sky notice Pippa was limping.

"I thought you said you were okay."

"A little sprain never killed anyone."

Nevertheless, he snaked his arm around her waist and cradled her against his side to support her. Her nearness took his breath away. He was definitely in love. In mad, crazy, gut-wrenching love. And nothing he could do would make the pain stop. He'd lied to her, and no way could he turn back the clock.

He wanted her, and from the way her green eyes seemed to melt as they met his, he guessed she felt the same physically, no matter what she felt for him otherwise.

Unable to tolerate the building tension, he sought to relieve it in the most basic way he knew how. He moved in on her. Slowly. Giving her the opportunity to shy away. He knew he was taking the chance of putting her off for good. But she didn't shy away; in fact, she met his gaze boldly, her breath catching in her throat.

He kissed her sweetly, hungrily, telling her without words what his heart wanted her to know. She moaned and moved closer, and he figured she was hearing him loud and clear.

Wanting to touch her intimately, burning to feel himself sheathed in her wet warmth, he crazily considered making love to her there on a sofa. On the rug. Mistake. A dead man's apartment. And an almost insurmountable issue still between them. He couldn't afford mistakes.

He made do with the kiss. And when he drew away, he asked, "Feeling any better?"

She swallowed hard. "Uh, right."

"I meant your ankle."

"I think it's swollen. I'll take care of it when I get home."

"Maybe you should see a—"

"No doctor."

He wondered if she was allergic to medical personnel or something. She certainly avoided them like the plague. Resigned that he wouldn't be able to talk her into anything but some self-help, he said, "Let's take care of it." He indicated the stools around the island counter. "Sit for a minute while I get some ice." Déjà vu. "You can doctor yourself on the drive home."

Home. Hers. A place he didn't intend to leave. He hadn't been kidding about being her shadow. Spending the night alone on one of her sofas might kill him, but he guessed he deserved it.

Pippa sat as he ordered, and Sky went straight to the refrigerator, feeling badly for her. First the blow to her head, then the bruised arm, now a swollen ankle. He hoped that that would be the extent of her injuries. The idea of something more serious happening to her because of their involvement in the investigation—*his* idea, for God's sake—wrapped an icy fist around his heart.

He was looking for a Ziploc bag in a drawer when he noticed some papers stuffed inside. The name *Acacia Fries* jumped out at him. Though Pippa had never told him Acacia Birch's maiden name, he knew no other woman with the unusual first name. The police must have missed this . . . if they even knew about Lamont's city residence.

He grabbed a Ziploc and filled it. "Here." Sky handed Pippa the bag of ice, while he looked over the papers.

Hanging on to the pack, she asked, "What's so interesting?"

He raised a hand to hold her questions and quickly scanned the document. It barely took a minute for the truth to hit him. "Acacia's not off the hook, after all."

"What do you mean?"

"Before he died, Birch must have been going over the terms of his wife's father's last wishes." He circled the counter and stood next to Pippa, ignoring the charge that shot through him. "The entire estate is in trust. Acacia had to marry within a year of her father's death or all the money went directly to charity."

"So she married Lamont."

"Right. She made her bed and that was that. Divorce was out of the question. Her father specified he wanted his daughter to be a 'seemly' woman, unlike her mother, who'd run out on them. Had Acacia divorced, the estate, again, would have gone to charity... but not if she were widowed."

"That's why she threatened to see Lamont dead before she gave him a divorce!"

"Exactly. So we have two distinct possible motives," Sky mused, weighing the possibilities. "An unknown woman wanting revenge for her mother's untimely death. And Acacia's wanting to retain her fortune, while being freed of a husband who was fooling around on her... with Valerie," he added, realizing he hadn't yet told Pippa about his heart-to-heart with the mayor's aide.

"Valerie Quinlan was Lamont's mistress?"

"Though not exactly by choice. Blackmail seems to have been his favorite game."

"Great. The plot thickens."

Did it ever. Two motives. Three suspects. If they hadn't missed something. Maybe a good night's sleep would shed new light on the situation.

Sky prayed something would click, for he was getting the feeling they were running out of time.

SHE WAS RUNNING out of time. The possibility of all that money slipping through her fingers made her physically ill.

Never! Not after what she'd been through in the past dozen years. Not now. Not when fate could so easily nail her again. Icing the shoulder bruised by whatever had hit her in the dark, she ruminated. How had things gone so wrong?

For one, she'd made the mistake of underestimating the McNabb woman at every turn. Under different circumstances, she might actually admire the little chit. As it was, Pippa McNabb was a liability. And Sky Thornton presented an even bigger one. Thinking of what might have gone down had he shown up even a minute sooner, she shuddered.

Regretfully, she would somehow have to take care of the unlikely couple in one fell swoop... would need to create a feat of misdirection that would allow her to get away with murder.

SKY HAD GOTTEN AWAY with murder the night before as far as Pippa was concerned. With the altered state of her nerves, she'd allowed him to prevail when he'd insisted on staying at her place for the night. So she'd remained sleepless for hours—tossing and turning, knowing he was on the couch directly below—only giving up the ghost shortly before dawn.

She'd been late to work, and now she was yawning her way through the day.

"I'm not keeping you up, am I?" asked Shelby, in whom she'd confided everything about Sky, but as little as possible about the danger she'd been in, and nothing about their theories concerning the murderer's identity.

In Pippa's office they shared a late-afternoon coffee break. Not that Pippa had done anything other than work an early catered lunch as scheduled. She'd had hours to brood since. She yawned again. "It's not the company, believe me."

"Although you'd probably prefer being with someone else."

Knowing Shelby meant Sky, Pippa protested, "I'm glad he finally went home."

Shelby's hazel eyes sparkled and her mouth bowed with suppressed laughter. "No, you're not."

"Well, part of me is."

"The part that wants to forgive him?"

"I guess. Shelby, what am I going to do?"

"Listen to your heart."

But her heart was confused. Sky hadn't simply held back some small detail from her. Being Dutch's brother, suspecting her of who-knew-what manipulations, searching for a nonexistent will—he'd kept major secrets. On the other hand, he'd had no reason to give a stranger his trust, especially not the widow of the brother who'd betrayed him. What a quandary.

She took a final, bracing sip of coffee and set down the mug. "I guess I'll have to listen awhile longer."

"Don't wait *too* long."

Wait. That's what Sky had instructed her to do when he'd finally left the store. She'd also promised to wait for her brother to bring her over to the temporary outdoor soup kitchen at the Daley Center. The food drive, sponsored by the Coalition to Feed the Homeless, would start this evening and last through the holiday weekend.

When Mayor Keegan had originally asked Sky to bring his reindeer to the fund-raiser, he'd also requested an appearance at the soup kitchen. Therefore, Sky would be giving homeless kids free rides around the perimeter of the block-square skating rink that lay between Westbrook's and Daley Center, and he didn't want her to be alone for a single minute.

Memories of her terror with the killer stalking her had prompted Pippa to promise.

"I'd better get back to work," Shelby said.

"At least you *have* work to do."

Pippa followed her sister-in-law out of the office and, on impulse, wandered over to Lamont's. She had to do something with the time until Rand came back from a meeting that was off the store's premises. Even though the police had been through Lamont's office, she might as well check out those papers in Lamont's safe as she'd thought to do the night before. Maybe something would click.

Zipping through the combination, she opened the safe and emptied it, spreading everything out on the desktop. Nothing triggered a response until she saw the envelope. Something made her pulse shoot through her unevenly.

And then she ripped open the envelope and read the contents, totally unprepared for one of the biggest shocks in her life.

STILL IN SHOCK several hours later, Pippa left the store alone, despite Shelby's protests. Rand was stuck in that meeting for who knew how much longer and she was too hyped-up to wait.

Fat flakes of snow drifted down from the heavens, ringing the streetlights with haloes and covering State Street with downlike fluff, the magical stuff of angels' wings.

"And all the angels in heaven shall sing, on Christmas Day, on Christmas Day..." came the strains of a nearby carol. Christmas might still be two days away, but this was a picture-perfect Christmas night.

Like the night of Lamont's death...

Pippa reminded herself to keep an eye out for anything dark and ugly prowling between the snowflakes. For who knew where the killer lurked?

Certain she would come face-to-face with at least two of their suspects this night—as the coalition director, Gwen would be visible, and as the mayor's aide, so would Valerie—Pippa remained alert as she crossed the street with hordes of other people. Many were the homeless souls who would be fed better tonight than they had been all year. She scanned their number, ever vigilant for a particularly short person in rags or a much taller one in a green hooded cloak.

No one to get her uptight, thank goodness.

She was tight enough as it was. The find in Lamont's office had propelled her onto the street alone in search of Sky. But try as she might, she couldn't spot him or his reindeer, either. Passing the outdoor ice rink, she took a better look, but saw nothing but people on skates whizzing by.

Counting on finding someone who would know where Sky was, she hurried toward the open plaza in front of Daley Center, ignoring the twinge of her wrapped ankle. Before the Picasso sculpture, long makeshift tables were being set with covered warmers holding food. The homeless were queuing for a plate of turkey and stuffing and mashed potatoes, ham and sweet potatoes and greens, pumpkin pie and cookies and bread pudding.

She scanned the crowd for a familiar face...and saw Gwen issuing directions to some of the workers. Boldly, though her heart was in her throat, she approached the other woman, hoping Gwen couldn't tell she was suspect. "Looks like the word went out to every homeless person in the city."

"I'm praying we don't run out of food tonight," Gwen admitted.

If Gwen had tried to kill her the night before, Pippa mused, could she really look her straight in the eye as if nothing had ever happened?

"You haven't seen Sky Thornton, have you?" Pippa asked, carefully watching the other woman's expression.

"Oh dear, he hasn't arrived yet?" Gwen seemed truly distressed. Her brow furrowed. "I hope nothing's happened to prevent him from coming tonight, or the children will be disappointed."

Pippa would be more than disappointed, but somehow she couldn't imagine Sky backing out of the agreement. "That would be terrible," she agreed, relaxing a bit and realizing that she was thinking of him as a man whose word could be trusted. "But he did say he would be here."

So what was keeping him?

Thoughtful, Pippa moved off when Gwen was summoned to take care of a problem. The soup kitchen had officially opened and people were being served, after which they sat to eat at the trestle tables lining nearly the entire plaza. At the opposite side, beneath the giant official city tree that was actually composed of dozens of smaller trees strung together, Santa Claus reigned. That gave her pause. A line of ragged-looking children along Clark Street waited for what probably would be their only Christmas present.

Drawn by the touching scene, Pippa wandered off in that direction. Santa spoke to a small girl and handed her a present. The girl hugged him, then ran off toward her waiting mother.

That's when Pippa spotted Santa's helper—a large child or small adult dressed like an elf. The helper chose a present from one of three piles—toys that would have been sorted into age groups, she guessed—and handed the gaily wrapped box to Santa. Her pulse kept time with her quickened footsteps as she approached to get a better look.

Suddenly the elf turned and, familiar gaze meeting hers, grinned sinisterly before taking off like a flash, keeping the line of kids between them.

"Hey, where are you going?" Santa shouted after him. "Who's gonna help me sort the gifts for the kiddies?"

"My friend here will help," volunteered an unlikely source—Acacia Birch, who was proffering her "dance instructor".

What the heck was Lamont's widow doing here?

Telling herself she couldn't worry about that now, Pippa took off after the dwarf, her pulse racing as fast as her feet. She tried to keep up with the man who'd followed her when she picked up the photos and again had appeared when she'd brought the folders to Gwen. Surely this could be no coincidence.

Surely he could lead her to the murderer.

Though hard-pressed to keep track of him over the heads of the kids, many of whom were larger than he, Pippa thought she was gaining on the man as they neared the end of the line. Then her foot hit a patch of ice. Despite her rubber-soled boots, she slid and teetered off balance, barely catching herself from taking a bad spill. Worse, she was distracted long enough to lose the man in the milling crowd. And try as she might, she couldn't catch sight of him again.

A hand clamped down on her shoulder. Pippa jumped, turned and squealed all in one shot.

"Hey, don't have a cow!" Mayor Keegan told her, appearing nearly as surprised as she.

Pulse jagging, Pippa said, "You startled me."

The mayor grunted. "What happened to Thornton?"

"What makes you think I would know?"

"I know lots more'n people give me credit for," the mayor told her, his expression crafty.

Boldly she said, "Then you know why Acacia Birch is here."

After cursing under his breath, he said, "Some things I miss."

So Acacia wasn't serving in any official capacity. Then why had she come at all? As far as Pippa knew, Lamont's widow had no personal interest in the Coalition to Feed the Homeless. Pippa was getting a weird feeling about this. . . .

The sound of murmuring across the plaza drew their attention. Above people's heads, Pippa could see, parked on the skating-rink side of Dearborn, the tops of the horse trailers Sky used to transport the reindeer.

How long ago had he arrived? she wondered.

"Finally," Keegan grumbled. "Where the hell is Valerie? Time for me to give my speech."

"It's a big crowd, but I'm sure you'll find her again."

"No *again* about it. She better show tonight if she knows what's good for her political career."

Acacia here, but Valerie not? What was going on? Maybe Sky would have some ideas.

After taking her leave of the mayor, Pippa first went back toward Santa to see what Acacia was up to. While Santa's new helper was being kept busy, Acacia herself was nowhere to be seen. Her heart thudded, and she had this funny catch every time she tried to take a normal breath. She looked over at the food lines. No Gwen, either. Swallowing was now nearly impossible.

Taking into consideration the fact that their three suspects might all be in the vicinity, if not visible, Pippa shot across the plaza, her thoughts in turmoil.

HER WORLD WOULD BE IN real turmoil if things went wrong now, she realized as she tightened her laces. Thank God Thornton had finally showed. This was her last shot at them. Too bad they'd forced her hand.

No one was supposed to get hurt other than Lamont. The bastard had deserved to die.

Knowing what she had to do was tricky wouldn't stop her. Nor would the fact that Pippa McNabb and Sky Thornton were innocent of any wrongdoing.

Once again, murder was a matter of survival.

Chapter Fifteen

Survival of the fittest. As she watched Sky and his assistant harnessing the team of reindeer from a distance, Pippa couldn't help thinking that they were engaged in a contest of sorts, trading wits with a very smart woman.

But which of the three was guilty? Acacia, Gwen or Valerie?

She crossed to the skating-rink side of the street. Gazing around as she headed down the sidewalk straight for Sky, who was now barely a half block away, Pippa faltered. For there, floating over the ice toward her came a dark silhouette—a woman wearing a long hooded cape. Even under the streetlights she could tell that the snow dusted a garment of green velvet.

Hers. The dead mistletoe mocked her.

She was nearly face-to-face with the murderer. As happened the night before, she couldn't actually see what lay hidden beneath the hood. But, creeping out from between the rich folds, a gloved hand motioned for her to come closer....

Without thinking, Pippa responded, changing directions, hurrying to meet the villainess head-on. She got onto the ice via one of several openings in the temporarily walled arena.

What could possibly happen to her with so many witnesses?

But as Pippa closed in on the cloaked criminal, she heard a familiar, taunting laughter. Again she faltered, her heart pounding right up into her throat. Was she as demented as the woman before her, purposely placing herself in danger? But how could she not respond to the challenge, when at last she had her chance to discover the murderer's identity? If she went for the police, their arrival would come too late.

This time, should she get close enough, Pippa vowed she would know her enemy. Then it would be all over but for the arrest.

"Who are you?" she shouted in vain. "What do you want with me?"

Getting close wasn't proving to be easy. For as Pippa carefully advanced over the frozen surface, keeping her balance by some miracle and despite her wrapped ankle, the cloaked figure retreated, gliding smoothly over the ice. *Skates!* The murderer was obviously wearing them. And Pippa realized it would take a miracle to catch up.

A miracle... unless she could figure a way to get the murderer off her blades.

As she neared the middle of the frozen arena, dodging a group of kids playing tag, it came to her. Pippa slipped off her shoulder bag and prayed all those years of lessons from Pop would pay off. She extended the bag in front of her, carefully took aim, swung her arm back then foward like a pendulum, then released it. The bag flew fast and low, the leather skimming the ice as smoothly as any bowling ball on an alley.

Though the other woman tried to get out of the way, she wasn't fast enough. *Strike!* Leather bag met skate. The murderer went down with a muffled scream.

Pippa slipped and slid forward, her adrenaline flowing as she quickly closed the gap between them. "Someone help me!" she yelled as she fell to her knees, then quickly scrambled up and forward. "This woman is a murderer!"

But rather than responding, nearby skaters avoided them. Either they didn't believe her...or they didn't want to get involved.

The other woman was up in a flash, but before she could skate off, Pippa firmly grabbed hold of the folds of the cape, then was frustrated when she heard a rip, saw the material tear. She refused to let the murderer get away so easily. Having played football with her brothers as a kid, she instinctively threw herself at the other woman in a low tackle, stifling the pain that shot through her still-sore arm on contact.

This time they went down together. More bruises. They rolled one over the other across the ice. Pippa snaked a hand up to the hood while the other woman fumbled with something near her waist. Pippa tore the hood free only to confront a face muffled by a scarf and knit cap drawn low. Several strands of dark hair clung to the silk. She searched for silver among the black strands to no avail.

"Gwen!" Pippa guessed, only to gasp when the other woman pulled out a hand to shove a gun in her face. "Or is it Winona Sarcosi?" she choked out for good measure.

"You're too smart for your own good, Pippa," Gwen said, rising to her knees and sliding back a little. "I knew you had the newspaper clippings Lamont saved all those years. Are they in your shoulder bag?"

"Look for yourself," Pippa offered, hoping to get the jump on the other woman once more.

Gwen reached for the leather strap blindly. "Get up." The gun disappeared into the folds of the cape. The shoulder bag followed. "And don't underestimate me."

Pulse throbbing with a combination of elation and healthy fear, Pippa weighed her options and figured Gwen really wouldn't shoot her with so many witnesses unless she forced the crazed woman's hand. They both got to their feet.

"What did I ever do to make you hate me enough to want to see me dead?"

"I don't hate you, that's the tragedy of this. But you know too much. If only you'd kept your nose to yourself . . . I really hate blackmailers."

"I can understand why you needed revenge against Lamont," Pippa said, trying to appease Gwen. And to stall her. Sky should be bringing his reindeer and sleigh onto the ice any moment now. "I read about your mother. I feel for you, going to prison because of the way you were forced to live."

"I'll never go back. I would rather be dead," Gwen said flatly. "After I got out, I tried to make an honest life for myself, but it wasn't easy with a record hanging over my head. That's why I changed my identity. Things were going great until I had the misfortune of running into Lamont Birch again."

"You weren't the only one Lamont was black-mailing," Pippa said, wondering what was taking Sky so long. "It was a way of life with him. What did he want from you?"

"Money." When Pippa looked at her questioningly, Gwen said, "I had access to coalition money, remember. First he insisted on several modest installments. Then he demanded enough to kick off his campaign for mayor in style."

Remembering her conversation with Acacia, Pippa realized it all made sense. "So that's how he planned to get the money."

"Luckily, we had lunch together at my favorite restaurant, and I learned he was allergic to peanuts. I made a few special appetizers for the party. He was so distracted, he didn't notice when I slipped them to him."

"But why involve me by using my cape?"

"That was impulse. I saw you arrive wearing it and knew that I could hide my identity, if necessary. You made it easy for me—you left the door open. So I guess you'll have to share the blame."

Pippa marveled at that twisted thinking. She also sighed in relief. At one end of the skating rink, she saw eight tiny reindeer and a sleigh being driven onto the ice.

"I set up a fake company," Gwen was continuing. "Even now the check is clearing."

Pippa's spirits rose. Help was on the way. "You were able to divert enough—"

"I took it all," Gwen admitted, also glancing over to the team traveling in their direction. "Ah, there he is," she said, her satisfaction sending a chill up Pippa's spine. "Tomorrow I'll be a rich woman. And I'm sorry to say you'll be dead."

Nerves twitching anew, Pippa said, "I'm not going anyplace secluded with you, so forget it."

"You're going to die right here, in front of all these witnesses. Another tragic accident. And Sky will then take the blame for both deaths . . . at least long enough for me to get away."

"Sky?" Pippa realized that Gwen planned on throwing her in front of the racing team, just as she had Lamont. She shook her head. "Sorry, Gwen." And reached out.

"What do you think you're doing?"

"This!" Pippa grasped the leather strap of her shoulder bag through the thick velvet and jerked Gwen off balance. The gun sailed right out of the murderer's hand and directly into the path of the oncoming team.

Expression truly demented, Gwen dived for the gun.

"Gwen, no!"

But, to Pippa's horror, Gwen kept going, crawling on the ice toward the weapon.

"Whoa, Dasher, whoa, Dancer, Prancer and Vixen!" Sky yelled, struggling to get the team under control. "Whoa, Comet and Cupid and Donder and Blitzen!"

Gwen's hand hit the gun, which went spinning farther out of her reach. Seeming to realize the mortal danger she'd put herself in, Gwen turned a horrified expression toward the flashing hooves and let loose a blood-curdling scream as Sky brought the team to a dead stop.

GWEN HAD SAID SHE'D rather be dead than return to prison. Staring into the fire, for a few minutes having her parents' living room to herself—the rest of the family was laying out the Christmas Eve buffet—Pippa was glad the murderer didn't get her wish. Then both she and Sky would have survived only to live with the memory of Gwen Walsh's death. She had enough on her mind—and heart—to live with as it was.

Gwen and her accomplice—the dwarf who turned out to be a former con man living on the streets—had both been locked up. After lecturing her about interfering in police investigations, Lieutenant Jackson had actually apologized for putting her under suspicion.

She and Sky had also informed him about the mayor's underhanded dealings with the City Streets complex. Jackson hadn't seemed surprised, making Pippa wonder if he hadn't discovered this information, as well, making him reluctant to *investigate* as ordered by the mayor. Perhaps he had suspected Keegan himself.

"Are you all right?"

Startled, Pippa turned from the fire to meet Shelby's concerned gaze. "Sure. Great," she lied for her sister-in-law's sake.

How could she be anything but awful when she didn't know where things stood between her and Sky? At least she now knew what she wanted...and she knew other things she'd been denying for too long, as well. So why hadn't Sky called?

"Your mom said dinner will be ready in five minutes."

"I'm not very hungry."

"Then eat for her. You know how she worries."

Pippa nodded. She put up a good front so she wouldn't ruin everyone else's holiday. "Five minutes."

Shelby had barely left the room before the doorbell chimed. The whole family was together. Who could be invading their Christmas Eve?

"I'll get it!" Pippa yelled.

A messenger stood on the porch, holding a small package and a clipboard. "Miss Pippa McNabb?"

"You've found her."

"Merry Christmas." He handed her the foil box and the clipboard.

She scrawled her signature on the appropriate line, fetched a couple of dollar bills from the vase on the mantel and gave them to the messenger. "Merry Christmas," she returned, wishing she could feel that way.

"Who is it, honey?" Pop yelled as she rested her back against the door and stared at what obviously was a present.

"Delivery for me." From Sky? "I'll be there in a minute."

Her hand shook as she undid the gold ribbon and opened the foil box. A slip of folded paper lay nestled in glitter. "For the Yule log," was written in Sky's hand.

Pippa swallowed. He remembered her talking about the tradition. Inside would be his most cherished wishes for the coming year. Heart soaring, she unfolded the list. A single word jumped out at her: *FORGIVE-NESS*.

She'd already forgiven him.

Thinking he should be here to throw this into the fire himself, Pippa wondered if he was. Breath caught in her throat, she opened the door. Sky stood on the other side.

"Can you?" he asked.

In answer, she fished in her pocket and brought out her own list for the Yule log. "That's what I was wishing for."

She, too, had only printed one word: *SKY.*

His mouth curled into that familiar smile. "So I'm here. Why don't you look happier?"

"Wait." Pippa pulled him into the room and toward the Christmas tree. "I have something else for you." Documents rolled and tied with a big red ribbon. "I found this yesterday, in Lamont's office safe."

Sky undid the ribbon. She watched his expression carefully; concern transformed to awe. "The missing will," he breathed.

"And it's signed. Lamont drew it up but never came forward. Maybe he was just waiting for the right moment to blackmail me." Then came the part she was dreading. "I was still married to Dutch, so he couldn't legally leave everything to you. I guess we'll be equal partners."

"As far as I'm concerned, there's only one way we'll ever be equal partners." He threw the will into the fire.

"What are you doing?" she demanded, watching the flames first lick the papers, then devour them.

"The only thing I cared about was getting my brother back, knowing that he still felt something for me, and now I know he did. As for being equal partners," he said, moving in on her, "that's still possible if you agree to marry me. Is it possible for us to start over?"

Pippa shook her head. "There's no going back. And I wouldn't want to. I've grown more in the past week than I have in a year. I want us to go on from here. Besides, from now on, I have my family to keep you in line."

She indicated the doorway where the entire McNabb clan had lined up, ten pairs of eyes watching with interest as an amazed Pippa was thoroughly kissed.

Merry Christmas to all, and to all a good night!

```
A  B  E  D  A  N  I  E  C  O  A  S  T  A
V  Q  U  A  L  Y  X  B  N  N  O  P  R  N
E  S  M  A  E  R  D  M  C  S  X  S  L  A
N  A  J  G  X  M  N  Q  O  E  O  E  I  M
G  E  A  E  A  I  E  U  M  N  V  C  S  E
E  S  C  R  N  E  S  W  Z  A  T  E  K  T
D  H  R  O  D  X  P  A  R  E  R  A  E  A
L  G  E  U  E  E  L  T  I  R  A  S  E  N
E  I  R  B  R  E  E  E  A  N  A  C  O  O
U  H  E  L  D  M  R  R  I  I  N  T  V  I
S  S  T  O  I  Y  K  S  L  A  D  E  B  S
H  C  C  T  U  W  V  I  M  R  P  I  H  S
Z  D  A  D  V  E  N  T  U  R  E  C  K  A
H  C  N  M  M  G  R  O  M  A  N  C  E  P
```

CLUES:

BREE	ADVENTURE	ALEXANDER
PASSIONATE MAN	TIME TRAVEL	SHIP
DREAMS	SCAM	AVENGED
COAST	HIGH SEA	WATERS
ROMANCE	SAILING	

WDF-3

Answers

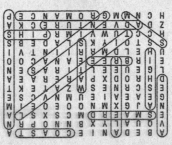

MILLION DOLLAR SWEEPSTAKES (III)

No purchase necessary. To enter, follow the directions published. Method of entry may vary. For eligibility, entries must be received no later than March 31, 1996. No liability is assumed for printing errors, lost, late or misdirected entries. Odds of winning are determined by the number of eligible entries distributed and received. Prizewinners will be determined no later than June 30, 1996.

Sweepstakes open to residents of the U.S. (except Puerto Rico), Canada, Europe and Taiwan who are 18 years of age or older. All applicable laws and regulations apply. Sweepstakes offer void wherever prohibited by law. Values of all prizes are in U.S. currency. This sweepstakes is presented by Torstar Corp., its subsidiaries and affiliates, in conjunction with book, merchandise and/or product offerings. For a copy of the Official Rules send a self-addressed, stamped envelope (WA residents need not affix return postage) to: MILLION DOLLAR SWEEPSTAKES (III) Rules, P.O. Box 4573, Blair, NE 68009, USA.

EXTRA BONUS PRIZE DRAWING

No purchase necessary. The Extra Bonus Prize will be awarded in a random drawing to be conducted no later than 5/30/96 from among all entries received. To qualify, entries must be received by 3/31/96 and comply with published directions. Drawing open to residents of the U.S. (except Puerto Rico), Canada, Europe and Taiwan who are 18 years of age or older. All applicable laws and regulations apply; offer void wherever prohibited by law. Odds of winning are dependent upon number of eligibile entries received. Prize is valued in U.S. currency. The offer is presented by Torstar Corp., its subsidiaries and affiliates in conjunction with book, merchandise and/or product offering. For a copy of the Official Rules governing this sweepstakes, send a self-addressed, stamped envelope (WA residents need not affix return postage) to: Extra Bonus Prize Drawing Rules, P.O. Box 4590, Blair, NE 68009, USA.

SWP-H894

THE VENGEFUL GROOM
Sara Wood

Legend has it that those married in Eternity's chapel are destined for a lifetime of happiness. But happiness isn't what Giovanni wants from marriage—it's revenge!

Ten years ago, Tina's testimony sent Gio to prison—for a crime he didn't commit. *Now* he's back in Eternity and looking for a bride. *Now* Tina is about to learn just how ruthless and disturbingly sensual Gio's brand of vengeance can be.

THE VENGEFUL GROOM, available in October from Harlequin Presents, is the fifth book in Harlequin's new cross-line series, **WEDDINGS, INC.** Be sure to look for the sixth book, **EDGE OF ETERNITY,** by Jasmine Cresswell (Harlequin Intrigue #298), coming in November.

WED5